**S**N LL

*Princess of Hell, #2*

# Eve Langlais

# COPYRIGHT & DISCLAIMER

1st Edition Copyright © January 2011, Eve Langlais
2nd Edition Copyright © November 2015, Eve Langlais
Cover Art by Amanda Kelsey RazzDazz Design © September 2015
Edited by Devin Govaere
Copy Edited by Amanda L. Pederick
Produced in Canada

Published by Eve Langlais
1606 Main Street, PO Box 151
Stittsville, Ontario, Canada, K2S1A3
http://www.EveLanglais.com

ISBN-13: 978-1518657641
ISBN-10: 1518657648

# CHAPTER ONE

The silence in Hell deafened me.

The screaming, the torturing, the day-to-day noise that was Hades, gone, and in its place, a deadly quiet that frightened me more.

I ran through empty streets where the buildings crumbled and leaned. Darted through the parks with the lava rocks and bubbling tar pools. I even hit the coffee shop that never closed, only to see nobody behind the counters, the coffee pots evaporated and dry. The horror.

Still running, I followed the winding path to the abyss, drawn to its ominous presence. I emerged from the towering stone walls that shaped the labyrinth to it and whirled around, searching the barren landscape that surrounded the gaping hole in the ground and found…nothing.

Not even a puff of wind. And yet, I couldn't shake the feeling I was watched.

Now usually, I was the type to preen if admired. *Stalk all you want, just don't forget to hashtag any stolen pictures. #1princessofhell*

I didn't get the impression the watching eyes belonged to my fan club.

It occurred to me that I should leave this place. Find my father, my lover, my friends, anybody. I'd even settle for that crazy bastard who'd told me I was the mother of all destruction. And I didn't even have to hire a PR firm to get that distinction, which totally miffed my father.

Who cared about my street rep, though, when there was no one around to admire it?

Or was there?

I took a single step and froze as I heard the faint scuff of someone approaching.

Suddenly, I wished for the quiet. Wished to be anywhere but here.

*Please not here.*

Without volition, I found myself pivoting to see a slight figure covered head to toe in a hooded robe. I'd seen scarier, and yet I whimpered.

Fear clutched me with icy fingers.

Dread sat its fat ass on my usually optimistic nature.

*Run!* I screamed at myself. Yet not a peep escaped my lips. Not even an atom of me moved because it was...

Too late.

My limbs betrayed me. Muscle turned to spaghetti, the well-cooked kind. I slumped to my knees, caught in the spell of the hooded one. My whole body trembled with fear.

How revolting. How unlike me. But I couldn't stop it.

In this moment, this awful moment, I, most awesome princess Hell had ever owned, was a victim.

A fucking victim!

It burned.

It disgusted.

I wanted to fight, yet my hands didn't move.

I wanted to run away, but the cowled figure held me frozen.

I wanted to plead for mercy, but no matter how much I tried, the words remained caught in my throat.

A good thing. I didn't think I could handle hearing myself act so weak.

The dark recesses of a hood hid the thing's cowardly face, and I wondered if perhaps that was a mercy. Did I really want to see the face of my nightmare?

It reached out a hand, the skin translucent and smooth, the tapered fingers perfectly manicured. Those innocuous digits approached slowly, and I felt tears leaking from the corners of my eyes, tears that burned as hotly as my shame. My breathing came fast and harsh. I anticipated the pain that was coming. I'd felt it before. Broken under it before. A pain so excruciating I would promise anything to make it stop. A pain so horrifying I wanted to die.

I'd tried once before, but failed. Hence why I now had to face *it*.

The hand hovered, a hairsbreadth from my trembling skin. So close… So close I couldn't help but let out a pathetic sound again. It was faint, but I heard it. And hated then mentally shrieked.

It touched me.

Immediately, the breathtaking torture started. Hot, lancing pokers ripped through my head and body. Unwavering, excruciating misery. I fell to the ground in convulsions, my voice finally free to scream, over and over and over.

A force grabbed my body and shook it. Pushed me down. Held me up. Rattled me again.

Along with the roughness, a voice penetrated the nightmare that clung to me tightly.

"Muriel! Wake up. Come on, baby, open your eyes."

Open them? And what, deal with reality?

*No, thank you.*

Yet I wasn't really given an option.

Someone just as stubborn as me wanted to force me to face the day. Only one man was brave enough to try and drag me from my terror-filled sleep. As Auric's strong arms wrapped around me, my horror-filled dream lost its grip. The nightmare didn't want to lose me though. It clawed at my mind, at what made me, me.

"Come back to me, baby. *Now!*" Auric wasn't the type to super mollycoddle me. He knew I didn't respond to weak kindness. He barked a command, and with a last, shameful whimper, I broke free of the nightmare. However, opening my eyes to morning sunshine didn't stop the shake in my limbs or remove the sheen of sweat. Waking up was all well and good, but the sharp memory of agony took longer to disappear.

And the shame always lingered.

"Oh, baby," I heard Auric whisper as he gathered me tightly to him and rocked me much like a child in need of comfort.

But I'm not a child. I am a woman. A strong one. The kick-ass bitch part of me demanded I push him away. After all, I held the title of princess of Hell. I should fear nothing and never show weakness. I didn't have nightmares. I gave them.

Unfortunately, I'd finally met someone who could give them back.

Ever since my encounter with the cowled being, I woke nightly screaming, announcing to the world my new cowardly nature.

Nothing I did made it go away. Nothing I punched. Killed. Drank. Or smoked.

And believe me, I'd tried. I had some pretty good connections when it came to acquiring mind-altering shit.

None of it even made a scratch in what I was going through.

It had been a month now, and every night, without fail, I suffered. And my shame grew.

Time to face the facts. I'd lost my edge. I now feared. I was no better than an ordinary *human.*

Disdain, a sin that was so easy to feel. And a great way to earn points with my dad. You know, Satan, the lord of Hell?

Hard to mock the weak when I was now one of them. My father, lover, and even my sister tried to reassure me that I'd gone through a traumatic experience and the nightmares were normal. They tried to tell me I was safe.

But I knew better. I knew they didn't understand. This creature still roamed the planes of Hell, Heaven, and the worlds in between. It was still out there. Even more frightening? It would come back for me. It hadn't found what it was looking for, the secret that hid inside my mind. It would return and try to rip the secret from me.

The old me would have bared her teeth and said, "Bring it on!" The new me cringed pathetically and, boy, did that piss me off.

The warm heat of my anger helped to burn some of my shame away. But even more heat came from the comfort of my lover.

Auric still stroked me, his caresses starting slow and sensual, the simple skim of his hands over skin soothing, and when my body relaxed, the touch became firmer. Bolder. More carnal. Yum.

Auric knew me so well. My very own fallen angel, and even more amazing, he loved me. Loved me even though I was a flawed product of Hell.

And I loved him back. From his gorgeous face with its rugged planes, heightened by a scar that gave rather than detracted from his beauty. How I enjoyed tugging at his silky ebony hair, thick and long enough for me to clench in a fist for a pull.

Yes.

Or instead of gripping his head to me, would I want him poised above, a tableaux to admire? He offered so much with his bulging muscles, wide chest, and a thick cock that knew how to fuck.

Crude. Perhaps. But sometimes sex was about being a little bit dirty. About feeling flushed and alive.

Like now. I needed to melt the chill from my body, and the most pleasurable way to do that involved Auric touching and claiming me.

A simple tilt of my face and he rewarded me with his lips, pressing them possessively against mine. Pure lightning at the contact.

Urgency exploded in me, and I kissed him frantically. To my carnal delight, he responded just as fiercely. Without saying anything, he gave me what I needed, a reassurance that we were both alive.

Alive and about to get lucky.

Gently, he rolled me to my back, but only so his body could cover mine. The friction of his skin against mine had me moaning against his mouth. Nothing like flesh-to-flesh contact. Two bodies as one.

His feverish skin melded against mine, warming me and moistening my pussy. But I needed more than just kissing and petting. I wanted his cock inside me, filling me up thickly, pounding and pumping until I indulged in a different kind of screaming. I also needed to recharge my magical battery that always seemed drained after one of my episodes.

Such a hard life I led, needing mind-blowing sex to tingle with power. The things I did. And loved.

I waggled my hips at him, my own hands

gripping at him, trying to pull him into me.

However, Auric had a different plan that didn't involve him pistoning me. He grabbed my hands and held them, pinning me to the bed.

A prisoner.

I trusted him, so I wasn't scared. On the contrary, my heart kicked up a notch. When Auric got dominant, pleasurable things tended to happen.

His mouth left my lips, and he worked his way down, the unshaven edge of his jaw dragging across the tender skin of my neck. He kissed me in the hollow at the base of my neck, such a vulnerable spot, before sliding lower to rub his face against my already erect nipples. He blew on my hardened nubs, all the while holding my hands down, even as I fought against his grip. I wanted to slide my fingers into his soft hair and force him to take my breast in his mouth. But I wasn't in control. Auric was, and he loved to tease.

He licked a wet trail around each of my nipples, his lower body pinning me down when I bucked. Finally, he sucked my breast into his warm mouth and let his tongue swirl around my nipple. A jolt of desire speared me between my legs.

I moaned and thrashed my head. Surely he saw how aroused I was? How much I needed to climax? Probably, but that didn't stop him from taking his sweet time, orally torturing each of my breasts in turn. "Auric," I said on a gasp as he nipped me. "If you don't make me come soon, I am going to hurt you."

And what did he reply to a threat that would have sent anyone else running and screaming?

He laughed, a purely masculine chuckle that made me shiver. "Impatient, my love? But I'm not done. I haven't had my morning honey yet."

With those titillating words, he slid down my body, his lips blazing a trail down my stomach to the curls he insisted I keep. My man was old school; he liked a landing strip. I didn't care so long as he kept visiting.

My legs already spread wide, I pulled at my knees, raising them that I might expose myself to him. It made me vulnerable, yet hot.

It showed my trust in him. It was also fucking sexy to watch. There he was nestled between my thighs. My heavy-lidded eyes met his smoldering gaze. As we stared at each other, he flicked out his tongue, and he gave me a long lick. I shuddered. I said a wanton, "Do it again," as I closed my eyes.

Thus did he begin the torture of my pussy, his tongue lapping alternately at my clit and between the moist folds of my sex. His fingers tightened around mine where he still held them, a sign of his growing excitement. Auric did so love to tease me.

He began exclusively flicking my sensitive clit, and I thrashed and screamed under his oral onslaught, my orgasm building inside. I reached the peak, but before I could tumble down into the abyss of pleasure, he stopped.

"Auric, please," I begged.

"Tell me what you want." His whispered words proved warm against my moist core.

"Fuck me," I said. "Fuck me hard."

Instantly, he lay atop me, my hands now stretched above my head, the head of his cock unerringly finding my wet passage and sliding in. I wrapped my legs around him, driving him in deeper. I loved the feel of his thick shaft inside me. Well endowed, he stretched me and had no difficulty touching the deepest part of me.

He claimed my lips, and I could taste myself on him. He pumped me, the hard length of his penis sliding in and out with steady strokes. Already so close to ecstasy, it took only a few thrusts before I screamed in his mouth, the blissful waves of my orgasm making me mindless.

Somewhere in the euphoric darkness that followed my intense pleasure, I heard him cry out, his body shuddering as he found his release inside me.

*Damn, I love wake-up sex.*

# CHAPTER TWO

Showered and feeling as if I could take on the world—so long as it wasn't wearing a stupid cloak—I perched on a stool in the kitchen and watched my man make me breakfast.

And, yes, this was better than any morning television show.

Dressed only in jeans, abs rippling as he moved, Auric tempted me more than the food he cooked—which smelled delicious. Were I not already running late for work, I would have gone for some sausage. But I was a responsible girl—most of the time—and I knew my belly needed nourishment if I was going to deal with the crowd we'd be sure to draw tonight at the bar. It was half off on drinks for witchy familiars. I truly hoped Greta showed with her bog troll. I'd ordered extra kegs just in case.

"I might not be able to make it in time for the bar closing." Auric announced this as he buttered some toast and handed it to me, along with some scrambled eggs.

"Your point would be?" I asked, arching a brow.

"Be careful walking home. Or, even better, call a cab."

Waste money so I wouldn't have to walk a few blocks? I understood why he wanted me to. I just didn't like it. "I am walking home. It's not that far. I know why you're worried, but might I remind you that we haven't seen a single demon since we laid the smackdown on that rebellion a little while back? And besides," I said with a lilt that held a hint of challenge, "are you implying I can't take care of myself?"

I'd put him on the spot and didn't feel the least bit bad. Auric needed to relax on the whole big protector thing. Things had actually been quiet since Hell's unexpected nap during the rebellion, meaning I hadn't had one single demon, shapeshifter, or other kind of assassin attack me.

One month and no attempts on my life? That had to be a record, and yet Auric still insisted I be walked to and from work. Like a baby.

"I didn't say you were a baby."

Oops. Had I said that out loud? Probably because I was tired of pointing out I could take care of myself. If only my blade could talk. My sword and I had spun a deadly tale over the years created from the blood of all the demons we'd dispatched. My sword could have told Auric he worried for nothing. "I can take care of myself."

"I know you can." He acknowledged my prowess and yet still pulled the overprotective bit.

My theory? He suffered from guilt. It didn't matter how many times I told him he wasn't at fault. He still hadn't forgiven himself for allowing me to be hurt when Hades had gone through its spot of trouble last month. The fact I'd traded my life for his also rankled. I think he was waiting for a chance to place his life ahead of mine so that he didn't feel in my debt. Never mind the fact that he'd traded in his chance to return to Heaven and brokered a deal with the devil to save my life. Nope, he just had to one-up me. Hadn't he realized yet that, if he did, I'd just do something crazier to get ahead again?

Silly really because, despite who did what, we'd won. Auric lived. I lived. The mysterious hooded stranger hadn't been seen or heard of since, and in the light of day, with the nightmare banished, I could even pretend it would never return.

And, besides, even if it did come after me, I'd blast him with my new superpower. My magic was stronger than ever with the daily multiple doses of sex Auric made sure I got.

Sex equaled power.

The knowledge still killed me, but then again, was I really surprised? Look at who'd fathered me.

My half-sisters were succubi, and my brother, well, we weren't too sure what he was other than the anti-Christ. He and Dad weren't really talking right now on account of he had *issues*. And, yes, I said that with giant air quotes.

But who cared about my boring brother? This was about me. Everything was. My daddy said so. Want to argue with the devil? Go right ahead. I tried that growing up. He took the term stubborn to new levels. Then again, stubbornness was a sin he'd created. Along with gluttony, greed, and lust.

And, boy, was I good at lust.

Just ask my boyfriend. Auric reaped the benefits of my voracious sexual appetite. It didn't bother him. He called it my nympho magic. The more pleasure—and orgasms—I had, the more powerful I became. I'd even begun suspecting that Auric's pleasure counted as well because if I happened to give him an amazing blowjob—apparently I had the perfect lips for it—I always felt a rush of power during and right after.

But knowing I was filled to the brim with sex and thus bursting with magic didn't stop Auric from pulling his macho routine.

"Woman, if I thought I could keep you safe in this apartment while I ran down the leads I dug up, I would."

"I'd like to see you try." Really I would. My smile was wide and the invitation for a wrestling match clear. Unfortunately, he didn't fall for it.

"Just be careful," he repeated. "Please." His green eyes peered at me with such love in them that I grumbled. After all, how could I retort in the face of such cuteness? Besides, while I could take care of myself, I loved that he treated me like a precious damsel who needed protection. Contradictory of me I knew, but still, I found it hot.

After a kiss that involved a lot of tongue and ass grabbing, I finally left for work, alone. Funny how Auric didn't worry about me getting to work during the day. Of course most demons and evil creatures tended to avoid daylight. How cliché since sunlight actually burned only vampires.

As I walked with brisk steps, Auric's words of warning stirring my mind, I thought over everything that had happened in the last few weeks. For one, I'd finally met the love of my life and gotten rid of my pesky cherry. My father was so proud. That Auric had turned out to be a fallen angel had been a bit of a shock at the time, especially considering he'd originally planned to kill me. But then he'd met me and fallen in love and decided to forgo Heaven in order to be with me. Nothing said true love like watching my lover choose eternal damnation to be with me. Of course, with my dad running things in Hell, the only way Auric would suffer would be if he hurt me.

And Daddy wouldn't have to help because I'd eviscerate him myself.

A little bloodthirsty? Fucking right. Didn't you know who I was? Satana Muriel Baphomet, the bastard daughter of Satan, and his favorite. A stately five foot nine-ish—and over six feet in my awesome stilettos—I have a lush figure with curves made for sinning and ass-length hair made for pulling. The dark color with its red highlights really contrasts nicely with my pale skin. As for my seemingly ordinary brown eyes, they light up with the flames of Hell when I'm annoyed. If Auric were here, he'd probably mention the fact that I have full lips made for sucking cock. And he would know since I loved going down on him.

I am twenty-three years old and madly in love—and horny—with my live-in boyfriend, Auric. My father was so proud I'd chosen to live in sin.

Speaking of Dad, I hadn't heard much from my father, Lucifer, since the incident in

Hell. I kind of missed his daily visits where I told him to get a life and stop stifling me and he said that half of my chromosomes belonged to him, and that meant he could pop in whenever he liked.

*I miss my dad.*

An admission that made me snort aloud. The people I passed on the sidewalk shot me a look and skirted around me.

I bared my teeth. Nice teeth, still, the crazy grin made them walk even faster.

Since I was thinking of my dad, I wondered if he had made any headway yet on the identity of the mysterious cloaked figure that tortured me. *Do we know who the asshole is?* I totally wanted him dead. Just the thought of that hooded being made me break into a cold sweat, even though the sun shone warm and bright.

Argh. My groan of frustration made some guy think I was hitting on him. He managed only to utter a, "That's it, darling, growl for— Oomph."

My blow to his diaphragm cut him short. He really didn't want to proposition me, not now that I was in a committed relationship. And in my current mood, the fact that he yelled, "Bitch, you're gonna pay for that," meant I didn't think twice about my long hair swirling in an arc as I thrust out with a foot in a nice roundhouse kick. He hit the pavement, and people walked around him.

Idiot out of the way, I went back to pondering my dad and the search for the cloaked dude. I knew Dad wouldn't rest until he found something out. As the Lord of Hell, he didn't like pretenders to his throne—*Lazy upstarts who think they can try and steal the empire I built,* he'd grumbled more than once.

As I neared the bar, my steps slowed, and I stopped. My pride and joy, Nexus, a tavern for magical and special beings, and I owned it lock, stock, and mortgage. Even better, I hadn't had to sell my soul to Dad for it. Being related didn't mean he hadn't tried, but I was wise to his tricks and had managed to keep my soul, thank you very much.

But back to Nexus. Originally, I'd wanted to make it a karaoke bar, but being practical minded, and with Auric's help, I'd opted to buy an LCD TV for my first big entertainment investment. I'd lost a lot of business during the previous season of *Survivor: Burn in Hell,* and I didn't plan to miss out when the next reality show, *Hell's Kitchen: Stay Out of The Pot*, started. I already had flyers done up promoting it and planned to start a betting pool on who would end up winning. I also looked forward to the next Damned Channel special event, *USS–Ultimate Soul Survival,* where the only rule was to stay alive. Watching the fights usually went hand in hand with copious amounts of drinking, and that meant money in my pocket. Ka-ching!

I did have a small dance floor where my special clients could rock to tunes on my jukebox, which had only hits from the eighties—a time when music didn't suck and love ballads made a girl wet her panties. Thankfully, my patrons put up with my eclectic tastes seeing as how I was the safest bar for supernaturals around. Of course it might have had something to do with the fact that most types of spelled magic wouldn't work around me, something to do with my special genes I was sure. Anyone who thought that wasn't a big deal had never seen a sorceress drunk on too many chocolate martinis. The term 'lightning bolts from her fingertips' often applied with charring results. Because of the magical void on my place, the worst anyone had to put up with were drunken covens singing off-key while their mascara ran, which, according to some people, was worse, but I digress.

I was proud to say my bar had become the hottest spot in and out of Hell—and places in between—for those that were special, AKA 'not human'. I had several staff members—dryads for barmaids, the more the better, as the concept of schedule and time didn't really work with them, what with their wooden skulls and all. Then there was Percy, my doorman and bartender. With the biggest hands of anyone I'd ever met, he knew how to straighten out those who thought they could get rowdy. Only idiots messed with giants, even half ones.

Until recently, not too many people knew of my title of princess of Hell. I preferred to go incognito. It saved on furniture, as the most common reaction to folks finding out my identity tended to be 'kill the daughter of Satan'. Like, hello, did it never occur to them to hate me on my own merit? Sometimes it sucked having a famous father, unless I wanted to skip the line into the Hellfire and Damnation dance club, then I totally name dropped.

Putting out bowls of Tabasco-flavored peanuts and napkins no one would probably use, I hummed away to the INXS tune of 'Devil Inside', not knowing my quiet life was about to change.

*Hours later…*

Exhausted, but a lot richer—the bar had sold an obscene amount of booze—I began my walk home. This was the first time since I'd met Auric that I didn't have company, and to my annoyance, I missed it.

Auric usually held my hand when we walked home, or on lucky nights, we flew. He might be a fallen angel, but due to a deal he'd brokered with my dad—where Auric actually kept his soul—he gained a pair of shadow wings. I loved it when he held me and swooped through the night like a dark knight preparing to debauch me.

Lost in my thoughts, I almost walked right into the trap, but luckily for me, the stench of demon acted like smelling salts. I snapped to attention. Scanning the darkness around me, the street lamps on this section of the sidewalk dead—or intentionally broken—I listened for a sound to tell me in which direction they would be coming.

I pulled my silver enchanted blades from my thigh holsters—never leave home unless armed—and palmed them. A quick chant invoked the fire within them, a magic bought from dragons and a magic so strong I couldn't negate it.

A whisper of sound behind me made me spin, my foot arcing out and connecting with something that grunted. As my opponent staggered, I popped into a ready position. Not really necessary, given I faced only a single demon. Piece of cake. Mmm…I wondered if we had any left in the fridge.

My lack of attention didn't mean I was oblivious to what was happening around me but at the same time, give me some credit. One bile-green demon was barely enough to make me break a sweat.

"Come on, ugly, let's get this over with. There's a chocolate cake with whipped cream icing calling my name at home."

The demon didn't seem in a hurry. He leered at me, pointed teeth gleaming, and whistled through their gaps.

Uh-oh.

It didn't need to hear the click of claws, or the whispery sound of leather wings dragging against buildings, to know my demon opponent wasn't alone. From the darkness, several demons emerged. All smiling. All eyeballing me like a fine piece of steak.

So much for going home and enjoying my cake. This would totally mean I'd need a shower because only savages and Amazons ate with the blood and guts of their enemy coating them.

What? Did I not show a proper concern for the enemy force facing me? Um, they'd sent only a half-dozen. I was *the* princess of Hell. They should have sent more.

Confidence didn't mean I didn't wish for my Hell blade. With my mighty sword, I would have sliced through their ranks like a knife through butter. Sadly, it didn't go well with most of my outfits, so I'd just packed my knives.

Hand-to-hand combat provided a great workout, but it wreaked havoc on my cleaning bill.

*Or if I get dirty enough, I could always go shopping.*

I'd stolen Daddy's credit card again, to his delight, which meant I could go shopping until it screamed.

Shaking out my wrists, my blades held in a reverse grip, I grinned, baring my teeth at the demons and beckoned them. "Here, pussy, pussies."

Okay, so I mocked them. Never show fear. Then again I didn't actually fear these demons. On the contrary, I could feel the adrenaline rushing through my body, and my eyes lit with the flames of Hell, a clue that usually meant get your ass out of my way.

But being stupid minor demons—the bile demons not high on any hierarchy ladder— they obeyed orders without thought. They tightened their circle around me.

Game on.

I didn't wait for them to attack. I moved first. More like danced, a slashing concert of death. I twirled and cut, slicing open demonic flesh, severing tendons, making them hiss and cry out as I showed them their mistake.

But there were quite a few of them. They surrounded me. When a meaty arm wrapped around my waist from behind and lifted me, my magic kicked in. Stupid and unpredictable, it only ever seemed to work when I was in dire danger.

Words of power filled my mind and rolled off my tongue in dark waves that spread from me and engulfed the demons. With shrieks and eyes that finally registered something—fear—they disintegrated into piles of ash.

Silence suddenly reigned, the only sign of the battle a sifting cloud of oily dust. Some of it got in my mouth, eeew! I coughed and fell to my knees, my body weak from all the magic I'd just expended. I heard pounding steps on the pavement and forced my head up in time to see a hooded figure jogging toward me.

*The cloaked one approaches. His hand stretching. Stretching…*

"No!" I cried out, the sound faint as fear stole my breath.

Panic set in, and already weak, my mind shut down.

Face, meet pavement.

# CHAPTER THREE

I awoke in a bed, not a coffin. Fist pump. Not a good sign was the fact that I didn't know how I'd gotten there.

Although, given I heard the rumble of Auric, I could wager a guess.

"I don't care what the fuck you do, but do something," Auric snarled, making no attempt to keep his voice low.

"I don't suppose anyone is in the mood to do me?" A rhetorical question. I knew Auric would give me what I needed, when I needed. And I needed now. Ugh. Even my brain was moving sluggishly.

My words didn't go unnoticed. Auric turned, his body taut with tension, and caught my gaze. I smiled. Apparently, I shouldn't have, as instant concern flooded his features.

"I gotta go. She woke up." He hung up the phone before he strode over to the bed, six-plus towering feet of masculine annoyance and worry.

"Are you okay? What the Hell happened?"

"Demons attacked. I fought back. No big deal. I obviously survived." And I was *hungry*.

29

Unfortunately, my boyfriend was in a mood to feed me a rant and not a certain part of his anatomy.

Auric raked his fingers through his hair. "Don't be so fucking nonchalant about this, Muriel. You're lucky David happened to come along when he did. And by the way, he's not impressed that you keeled over face first on the pavement when you saw him."

I winced as I remembered. I wanted to blame my swooning bit on my depleted strength from the fight, but the truth? The damned hood had sent me into panic mode, and I'd fainted like some pussy little girl. Not that I'd tell Auric that of course.

Being Daddy's girl, I lied. "I used more magic than I should have and passed out. I'll be more careful next time."

"Next time? Next time!" shouted Auric. "What if it hadn't been David who came across you? What if it had been another demon? You could have died."

"Well, I fucking didn't!" I yelled back, ruining my stance by having to close my eyes as waves of dizziness took control of my body.

The mattress sank under Auric's weight as he clambered into bed with me and scooped me into his arms.

"You fucking idiot," he said, but with affection.

"I didn't do it on purpose." Because if I had, I would be gloating. I liked to own my actions.

"I know you didn't." He hugged me closer and sighed. "I'm sorry I freaked, but I blame you."

"Me? I was the victim."

"Exactly. When David carried you in, all pale faced and with blood on your forehead—"

"How badly did I whack myself?" My hands patted my skin.

"Just a scratch, but it looks worse. You looked like a bloody corpse."

"A sexy corpse, as in undead vampire or ugly, nasty one like brain-seeking zombie?"

"This is not a joke, baby. Seeing you like that scared me. I love you."

Warm, mushy feelings invaded me. I did nothing to stop their assault. "I love you, too. Now can we stop yacking and get to the part where we kiss and make up? I could use some loving to get my magical reserves back up."

"We need to talk about what happened."

"Why bother? We both know what you're going to do. You'll demand I don't go anywhere alone. I'll laugh. Maybe mock you. You'll threaten to spank me."

"I'll do more than spank you," Auric growled. "I'm going to chain your sweet ass to this bed."

"Sounds like fun. But it's totally impractical because you know you can't keep me a prisoner here forever. So, instead, the times you can't act as my personal bodyguard, you'll probably assign David or Chris to chaperone me around."

"And you will cooperate," he added.

I snorted. "Good luck with that." I didn't plan to give in easily, no matter how right he might be. Yes, it was a dangerous time for me right now. Yes, there were things about my magic that needed explanation. However...my freedom meant a lot to me, and I refused to live a life of fear.

*I won't be a prisoner...unless it's for erotic purposes.*

"This isn't over, Muriel." Auric tried to use his stern voice on me. Deep, commanding, sexy. I loved it.

"Forbid me again," I whispered as I maneuvered myself so I straddled his lap.

"What am I going to do with you?"

"Wicked things." Starting right now. As I squirmed in his lap, I latched my lips to his neck and sucked.

"No more leaving this house alone," he ordered, even as his hands gripped my ass cheeks and pressed me harder against him.

"We'll see." I then decided we'd talked

enough and started a sensual fight with my tongue.

My skirt rode up, leaving me astride him with only a skimpy pair of panties. I fumbled with the buttons on his jeans, mewling in frustration against his mouth when I couldn't free his cock fast enough.

Auric dumped me on the bed and stood up to shuck his pants and shirt, the long length of his cock jutting proudly from his body. I smiled at him and moistened my lips. With a growl, he divested me of my clothes, not bothering with zippers, just tearing them from my body until I lay there as nude as him.

"Come here." I crooked my finger at him.

With a smile that made me shudder and flooded my lower regions with wetness, he lay down. I loved looking at his body—thickly built and bulging with muscles.

I straddled him, poising my slick sex over his straining cock. I grabbed my tits and squeezed them for his visual enjoyment and lowered myself onto him, impaling myself on his length. I threw my head back at the feel. Exquisite.

The cowgirl position made him go so deep, and I loved it. I leaned slightly forward and braced my hands on his chest and squirmed on him, the swirling motion making him catch his breath and making me close my eyes in pleasure. The tip of his cock rubbed against my sweet spot inside, and as I gyrated faster, his hands gripped me around the waist to help me. I dug my fingers into his chest, moaning as I rode my wild stallion. I could feel my orgasm building, the muscles in my pelvis tightening around his rigid length. Throwing my head back, I screamed as I came, the waves of bliss making me limp. Auric flipped me onto my back, never pulling out, and as I throbbed around him, he pounded me, hard and fast. He leaned forward and caught one of my nipples with his lips and sucked. Already in the throes of an orgasm, I was hit by another, and I screamed again as he came with a bellow of his own.

I'd like to say we spooned afterwards and said I love yous, but quite honestly, exhausted and sexually sated, I passed out.

# CHAPTER FOUR

Don't touch me. Don't touch me.

Noooooo!

I woke from the nightmare, tears rolling down my cheeks, my chest tight with sobs of anguish.

Auric spooned around me. He held me tightly and rocked me. "Shh, baby. You're safe."

I was pathetic.

Once again, I'd let a nightmare reduce me to a puddle of fear. Angry, and desperate to erase the nightmare, I turned in Auric's embrace and found the soft skin of his neck and sucked it. The salty taste of his skin brought me back to reality and made me horny.

I nudged my hips against him in invitation, too impatient for foreplay. He'd nudged my wet cleft with the swollen head of his shaft when I caught the familiar stench of brimstone. Auric rolled out of bed, his holy sword in hand, his naked—still erect—body a thing of beauty as he stood ready to defend me. I, on the other hand, didn't panic. I knew of only one demon that could get through the spells that protected our home.

Daddy had arrived in his usual peremptory manner that didn't involve knocking or warning.

"Hi, Dad." I imbued all my annoyance and sexual frustration into those two words.

My father, the king of Hell, stood with his back to us in our living room, a room we could clearly see due to the open nature of the loft apartment we lived in.

"Muriel, Auric, so glad you're up," said my father with too much glee.

"Now there's an understatement," said Auric, leaning over to whisper in my ear naughtily.

I giggled. His shaft still stood at attention as he sheathed the sword—the real one and not the one between his legs. Apparently it would take a lot more than a visit from my father to dampen his ardor.

"I can hear you," sang my father. "If you two want to finish up, I can wait. I'll just sit here and watch some TV. Don't mind me. I won't be listening at all."

Auric's body shook, and a glance at his face showed him trying to control his mirth. If I wasn't afraid my father would stand over us giving pointers, I just might have gotten my morning nookie. I had a hunger in my body that had nothing to do with food. I also knew, once I got out of this bed, I wouldn't be able to satisfy that craving until much, much later.

Auric turned his back to me, a flash of naked butt taunting me before he pulled on a pair of track pants. With a sigh, I flung back the covers and grabbed my robe. Belting the silken material around my curves, I walked barefoot over to my father and kissed him on the cheek before heading to the kitchen to grab a cup of coffee, freshly brewed with our Keurig.

"So what brings you here so bright and early?" I asked. I sipped the hot java while eyeing with interest Auric's naked chest while he puttered around the kitchen making us some toasted bagels. I didn't cook—unless it was trouble. My lover, on the other hand, could, both in and out of the bedroom.

"I've had my scientists and mages working on that sleep incident."

More than an incident. A month ago while Auric had been tortured at the hands of a major demon, Azazel, and his mysterious hooded master, all of Hell had been put under a massive sleep spell. Millions upon millions of the damned, demons and everything in between, including my father, had fallen victim to it. I'd noticed the spell when I'd gone to Hell on my rescue mission, but had not realized just what it meant at the time. Not a pleasant day when all was said and done. I had managed to save Auric, trading myself for him, only to be tortured magically and mentally to within an inch of my life. A torture I relived every single night.

"What have they found out?" I asked, my tone subdued. I still didn't like to think about that dark time.

As if sensing my disquiet, Auric came up behind me and wrapped me in solid arms. I leaned into his strength.

"It's bad."

For the first time I'd ever recalled, my father appeared shaken, which, in turn, frightened me. If Satan feared, then we were in big trouble.

My father rubbed at his face, impeccably shaved as usual. "Remember how I said a bunch of the damned seemed to be missing after that debacle?"

I vaguely remembered, but I'd been more interested in banishing the memories and discovering the pleasures that could be found with my new boyfriend at the time. "Did you find them?"

"Not really, but we did find out what happened to them. Turns out they weren't just missing. They're gone. Vanished. Not a trace of them left behind."

I frowned. "What do you mean gone?

Did they find some way to escape to the mortal plane?"

It didn't happen often, but some of the wilier denizens of Hell did make their way Earth-side.

"No. They're gone gone."

"Did they all jump into the abyss before or after the spell that put you to sleep?"

The abyss was where the damned who'd done their penance went to have their energy, their souls if you will, recycled so they could be reborn. Surprisingly enough, many souls chose to live in Hell instead of taking that final leap and losing their identity for good. Something about the finality in dying again really wigged them out.

"I don't get it. So a couple of souls got freaked and leaped into the hole for some reincarnation. What's that got to do with the big nap everyone took in Hell?" And why did he care? Fewer souls meant less paperwork. Something my dad usually applauded by taking the day off to play a round of golf.

"We're talking about more than a few souls, my daughter. Try six hundred and sixty-six thousand, six hundred and sixty-six."

That was a lot of sixes, not to mention kind of cliché. "Are you sure?" I asked incredulously. That was a pretty damn big number of people to have disappear all at once.

"Very, we've counted quite a few times. Each time it comes out to the same. Not only that, but they've been wiped clean. As in not recycled in the abyss, as in will never be reborn again. Gone."

"But how?" Then, in one of my rare moments of insight, I got it. "The sleep spell was powered by the souls of all those people." Horror made my jaw drop and my eyes widen.

Don't get me wrong. I was an evil bitch who didn't hesitate when it came to striking a killing blow. But that was face-to-face, straight-up battle. A spell that blindly stole souls to power it went beyond evil into...I didn't have a word for it. It was that fucking wrong.

"Someone out there has found a way to use the damned," said my father grimly.

"But who?" I whispered. Who had the knowledge and power to do something so horrible? And why?

Auric had a theory. "I have a feeling that Azazel's master, the robed one that tortured you, was behind it."

The mention of that bastard made me shiver, and that really annoyed me. In the light of day, I knew the only reason that cowardly robed being had managed to hurt me was because of the 'I won't fight you' deal I'd brokered to secure Auric's release. Had I not been magically bound by the terms of that agreement, I'd have let my blade taste that supernatural's blood.

And you will still drink it, my precious. My blade and I had a date with a certain asshole. Maybe if I decapitated the freak, the nightmares would stop.

"But why?" My father was the one to ask. "What purpose did it achieve in putting us all to sleep for a bit?"

Judging by my father's arched brow and Auric's glance at me, they both thought his last question was significant. So I backtracked and processed the words, but I still didn't get it.

It wasn't the first time I'd ever gotten the impression there was something right in front of me, jumping up and down waving for my attention, that I just couldn't see.

"Think, Muri," my father cajoled. "Use that pretty head of yours for something other than a hat rack."

Me, wear a hat? Never. I didn't have the right shaped skull for it.

Auric growled. "That spell was never about striking a blow at Hell or your father. With everyone in the pit so vulnerable, why didn't this mysterious master kill your father?" More than brawn, my lover had brains, too.

And hearing his question made me want to slap myself for missing it. It now seemed so obvious.

"I am not that easy to kill." Daddy crossed his arms and looked a tad disgruntled at the suggestion.

"No, you're not," Auric agreed. "But admit it. While you and everyone else was in drooly happy land, anyone could have walked in and put you in chains, or taken your head, or…"

"Dressed me in a sequined evening gown and put makeup on me. Not that it's ever happened before." The innocent whistle and stare at the ceiling failed.

But I wasn't interested in my father's drunken escapades. I tried to grasp what was more important than scoring one over dear old dad. "What could have been more important than Daddy's death or the takeover of Hell?" I couldn't stop a shiver, and even the safety of Auric's arms couldn't chase the chill.

"Do you really need to ask?" was Auric's soft query.

I knew what he was implying, but I didn't want to think it. *But you have already wondered. Wondered if it will come back to finish the job.* The robed one wanted something from me, something I firmly believed he'd not gotten, and if it was truly important, and I had over sixty hundred thousand vanished souls that said it was, then that monster would come back again. He would come back to finish the job. Finish me. Transport me back to that world of pain.

*Noooo.*

Even thinking it made me whimper. Auric kissed the top of my head, and I saw a flash of pain cross my father's eyes. Satan might be the king of evil, but he was also my daddy. I knew he loved me—even if he never said it—and it drove him nuts that something had hurt me. Something dared to harm his little girl and he hadn't been able to punish it yet. Daddy was a strong believer in tit for tat.

"We don't know that it was specifically after you," said my father, spinning a white lie that I could tell even he didn't believe.

"Don't treat me like I'm an idiot," I said, pushing away from Auric's comfort. I also pushed away the fear that kept trying to take over my body. I refused to be afraid. "They obviously didn't want Auric. They traded him for me. They didn't want you. They left you snoring and drooling on your throne. They wanted me. I'm not stupid, so stop pussyfooting around the fucking issue. That fucking asshole wants me!" I screamed.

Okay, I admitted to losing a little bit of control there, but anger burned a lot more cleanly in my psyche than that wretched stifling fear I kept suffering from.

"We don't know that for—"

I cut Auric off. "I appreciate you trying to lie to me, but let's face facts. They didn't get what they wanted the first time. Something more than just my power. They wanted something hidden in my head. Mind telling me what it is exactly, Daddy Dear?"

Lucifer shifted nervously. "I don't know."

I hated it when people lied to me. "Daddy, it wanted my memories from before I came to Hell. From when I still lived with my—" I had to force the word out. "Mother." And even as I did, I felt a stab of pain in my head for the woman who had callously dumped me.

"I'm sure you're mistaken," my father said too quickly.

"Really? Then why is it my memories from that time are locked up tighter than a virgin in an iron maiden chastity belt that's been welded shut?" I had always had a way with words.

"I don't know. For your own protection maybe so you wouldn't remember and pine for something that could no longer be."

I frowned at my father. What a load of bullshit. "What the fuck are you hiding?"

I could see my father grimace, and he shrugged instead of answering.

"Okay, let's look at this a different way. Why would this creature be interested in my life as a child? We're missing something here."

Trust Auric to once again see to the heart of the matter. "Who is Muriel's mother?"

It seemed so simple. So elegant. So obvious. So why hadn't I thought of it? Actually come to think of it, why had I never asked my father about the mysterious woman who birthed me? I tried to recall one single instance where I'd questioned my father about my absent mother and realized I hadn't. I'd thought of her over the years, cursed her many a time in my head, but not once had I ever voiced my questions about her aloud.

I forced myself to say the word mother again, my throat tight. "Mother." Again I felt that stab of pain. I turned stricken eyes to Auric. "Auric, I think I'm under a spell. I can't seem to—" The words had to be forced past a suddenly thick tongue. "Ask questions about my m-m-mother."

Just saying this much sent a much larger jab of pain through my mind that had me sinking to my knees, grabbing my head with both hands.

"Muriel." I heard the concern in Auric's tone, felt him kneeling beside me, as I rocked on my knees, working through the pain that shot through me and left me a trembling wreck.

"What have you done to her?" Auric said harshly.

"Why does everyone always blame me?" grumbled my father.

"Because you're the devil."

"Good point. And in this case, true."

"What's true? What did you do?" Auric snapped.

"I did nothing except prevent that whole head-might-explode thing from happening," replied my dad. "When Muri came to me as a little girl—"

Auric interrupted. "What do you mean came to you as a little girl?"

"It was the strangest thing. I woke up and there she was sitting on the foot of my bed, hugging a stuffed bunny, staring at me."

"He screamed," I added, ignoring the baleful look of my father.

"I was a tad startled."

So startled he shrieked in a pitch usually reserved for women, but I kept that to myself.

"How did you know she was your daughter if you'd never seen her before?" Auric asked.

"A father knows," the devil said sagely.

I snorted. "He yelled, 'who the fuck are

you freaky child?'"

"An understandable statement," my father replied with a sniff. "And that's when Muri said, 'you're my daddy'."

"And you believed her?"

"Of course not." My daddy snorted. "Do you have any idea how many females have claimed over the centuries they've born me a child? I immediately demanded a blood test, but I knew before the results came back she was mine."

"I have Daddy's eyes." It took only one tantrum by me, where my eyes glowed with the fires of Hell for my father to realize, I truly was his daughter.

"What of her mother? Who was she? Why did she dump Muriel on you without so much as a word?"

To that query, my father shrugged. "I haven't the slightest clue, and I tried asking. But Muri could tell us nothing. She couldn't remember her life before coming to me, or her mother."

"And what of you?"

At Auric's foolish question, I snickered. "You're asking the biggest manwhore if he remembered a possible one night stand, among dozens—"

"Hundreds," my father interjected.

"—that created me? Seriously?"

"I didn't know who Muri's mother was, but she was mine. And I decided to keep her. But my daughter has a bright mind, she takes after me don't you know. Even though she didn't recall her mother, it didn't take her long to realize that other children had a mother. The first time she asked me about her mother, she was in bed for three days screaming."

"What of when you questioned her?"

"Strange thing that. It was as if she never heard us ask. But, when she finally started to question, she'd go into horrible shrieking fits. It happened each time she dared to question about *that woman*." I peeked through my fingers and saw the moue of distaste on his face. "There's a geas on Muri, actually there are several. The spells are layered and impossible to remove. We've tried."

"What spells? Why did you never tell me about this?" I was astonished to discover my father had kept such a secret from me.

"Because telling you would have made you question, which would have caused you even more grief."

"What do the spells prevent Muriel from doing?" Auric asked.

Daddy held up a finger. "First, she can't ask about her mother without experiencing pain. She would say it, and boom, she was clutching her head screaming. Little girls have shrill voices you know. I couldn't stand to listen to it."

Lie. My father couldn't stand to see me in pain. But admitting it would alert folks to the fact he cared about me. What a goof. People already knew that, but if it made him happy…

"When I realized what was happening, I had a small compulsion placed on her, one that would get her to avoid asking questions about her mother aloud, which seemed to be her biggest problem."

Talk about learning something new. No one had ever told me about the geas placed on me in regards to my mother. A geas was a spell or, in many cases, a curse, that compelled a person to act a certain way or experience things if specific conditions were met. In my case, mommy equaled pain.

"Who is her mother?" asked Auric, saying the words I couldn't.

"Did you not pay attention, boy. I don't know."

"Bullshit. She was obviously someone powerful. I mean, look at Muriel. She isn't like everyone else."

Unique, that was me.

"No shit, but I'm telling you I have no idea."

I felt Auric's hold tighten around me, my father's evasive answer angering him. "This obviously all centers around Muriel's mother. So why are you protecting her instead of your daughter?"

"I'm not. I just can't tell you. I know she had a mother. I know she was powerful. But other than that, I can't tell you her name or even what she looks like. My memories are just as blank as my daughter's."

"Liar."

"I wish. In this case," my father grimaced, "I'm telling the truth."

That slammed Auric's mouth shut and stunned me. Who had my mother been that she had the strength to mess with my father's mind? Come on, my dad was Satan. King of Hell. Nobody, not even his brother, God, could mess with him. But apparently my so-called mother could. And…

"The cowled figure? It had power. Lots of it." I pushed out of Auric's arms and paced. "What are the chances of two people being interested in me like that?"

"You think it might have been your mother? Was it a woman?" Auric asked.

I thought of the hand, slim, pale and almost delicate looking. "It could have been. I don't know. All I ever saw was its hand."

"But why?" My father paced and, in the blink of an eye, grew a goatee, one that he could stroke thoughtfully. "Let's say it was your mother for a minute. Why hurt you sifting for memories? She placed the spell on you, so she should be able to remove it."

"I don't know." Maybe she forgot. Maybe she just didn't care. But I was more determined than ever to find the cloaked stranger because, if it was my mother, she had a lot of questions to answer. Right after I popped her one in the nose for fucking with my head in the first place.

We hashed it out a little more without coming any closer to an answer. My father left, yet the whiff of brimstone, his calling card, wafted behind. Annoyed and feeling sticky, I hopped into the shower as Auric made a few calls.

As I soaped my body, I waited for him to join me. I loved the feel of his hands on my body. It took very little thought—and touching of myself—to bring myself back to a fever pitch. I leaned against the shower wall and closed my eyes, rubbing my hard clit and imagining Auric on his knees, his tongue lapping at me.

As if conjured by my fantasy, I felt motion. I opened my eyes to see him smiling at me wickedly.

He knelt in the bathtub, his hands gripping my hips. I propped one leg up on the side of the tub and grabbed his hair, pushing his face toward my cleft. With a strength I loved, he held back so he could tease me, holding his lips just close enough to my sex for me to feel his warm breath tickling it. My pussy contracted in anticipation. With a light flick of his tongue, he touched my nub. My body shivered. He stroked it again, the back and forth wet laps making me dig my fingers into his scalp, urging him on. He placed his whole mouth on me and sucked, his tongue delving between my velvety folds and stabbing me inside.

I could hear myself moaning, my body building itself up to a fever pitch. When he tore his mouth away from me, I whimpered with loss. But I knew what was coming.

Auric wrapped his arm around my waist and lifted me enough that I could feel the tip of his erect cock probing my wet sex. I wrapped my legs around his waist and my arms around his neck and sheathed him inside me, loving the feel of his thick shaft sliding in and stretching me to accommodate his width.

With his hands gripping my ass cheeks, he pumped me under the pounding hot shower. The water made it seem tighter as it washed away my natural lube, but I enjoyed the gripping feel as he had to push his cock hard to get in. My whole body panted in time to his rhythm. My nails dug into the skin of his shoulders as he brought me to the edge and, with a hard thrust, brought me over it to fall, diving into the pit of pleasure that first made me feel weak then so incredibly strong.

He slipped out of me but still he held me. One hand left my ass to fumble with the soap, only to return as he lathered my bottom, his touch sending little aftershocks through me. I let my legs slide down and stood shakily, leaning into him. I loved it when he bathed me. And had I not needed to get ready for work, I would have taken him back to our ginormous bed and shown how much I liked it by fucking him with my mouth until his eyes rolled back in his head.

Hmmm. Now that I'd thought of it, I'd definitely have to indulge in that later. I whispered what I wanted to do to his cock after work in his ear, the look of torture and anticipation on his face making me already count the hours until I could make it a reality.

But Auric had mastered the art of teasing long before I had. Almost dressed for work, I turned around to see him fully clothed, sitting on the bed, pants unbuttoned with his cock in his hand.

My body flushed with desire. "What are you doing? You know I don't have time. I've got to get to work."

"I know," he said, rubbing the blushing

tip that I loved to lick. "But you got me so horny that I thought I'd show you just how much. And, while you're at work, I'm going to be thinking about you while stroking my cock and…"

I dove, my lips seeking that swollen Popsicle, but he held me off, laughing. "Nope, no sucking until later. In the meantime, you can just think about it."

I hated it when he turned the tables. I hated his laughter even more as I swapped out my wringing wet panties for dry ones. Jerk.

Finally dressed, we left for the bar. Auric seemed distracted by my side and didn't say much. I couldn't complain too much because, as per his habit, he held my hand, an old-fashioned gesture that should have never gone out of style. I preferred it when we flew—his gorgeous shadow wings making him seem so much bigger and badder—but he reserved that special treat for late at night when normal people slept. I still hadn't managed to convince him to have sex while in flight, but I hadn't given up yet. Too distracting, he argued. Bah. I thought the fact that we could crash added an element of spice.

"A blowjob for your thoughts?"

"Hmmm." My words startled him, and he gave me a smile that was just a façade. It didn't reach his eyes. "Nothing important. Just thinking about some stuff."

I hated it when he gave me vague answers. It usually meant he was pulling the overprotective routine, the one that implied that, as a female, I should be sheltered. Cute, kind of hot, but so annoying because I hated to be kept in the dark. I could have let it bother me, but I knew I'd wheedle it out of him when he was ready. Besides, I was pretty sure he was still stuck on the conversation we'd had with my dad earlier.

"So any ideas on who donated my X chromosomes?" I asked, pleased with my roundabout way of asking about my mother that didn't cause an instant brain aneurism.

"I've been thinking about it since your dad left actually. I've got a few ideas, but I want to do some research before I say anything."

I rolled my eyes. Him and his research. I preferred the more direct approach—shove a sword under someone's throat and make them talk. Of course, we'd need someone who actually remembered my mother for that to work. Damn it, there went that bright idea. I guess we'd have to rely on his plan to Google his ass off looking for answers.

We reached my work, and I yanked my pensive boyfriend into the alcove and planted a big wet one on him. That brought his thoughts back to where they belonged—on me!

His hands roamed over my back and slid down to cup my ass. His big hands squeezed my rounded tush and made my breath come faster. I ground my pelvis against his, thinking longingly of the couch in my office in the back. Maybe a quick—

A whisper of sound behind my back and I found myself neatly stowed away behind Auric's solid form. I heard the snick of a blade being pulled from a sheath.

"Would you put that thing away?" I hissed in his ear. "It's still broad daylight."

"And Charon should know better than to sneak up on us," growled Auric, sliding his blade back home. I knew another blade that wouldn't be getting slid home now though. Stupid clients interrupting my plans to slack off at work.

But at least this client I liked, so he'd live.

"Why are you sneaking up on my boyfriend?"

"Sneak? Not my fault the boy was so busy sticking his tongue down your throat that he didn't hear my approach."

"Maybe if you walked like a normal person, he'd have heard you."

"Why walk when you can glide?" Charon chuckled, the sound floating out from the dark recesses of his hood.

A little shiver of fear went through me, a shiver that pissed me off since I'd known Charon forever. He was an old friend of my father, practically my uncle, and furthermore, I knew he had nothing to do with the other hooded stranger.

"Is something wrong?" I asked, leaning against Auric and stalling with chitchat to keep him by me a moment longer.

"I need a drink. Bad."

"Why? What happened?"

Charon, the ferryman of death, sighed. "My son somehow managed to put a hole in my favorite boat, so it's in the shop being repaired. I've got the night off, but I'll be working twice as hard tomorrow bringing the damned down the river."

I choked my giggle back. A month back, Charon's son had dropped the oar in the river Styx and stranded his passengers—the new damned souls for Hell. Poor Charon. I was beginning to get the impression his son would not be following in his shoes… er, robe.

Something buzzed at my hip, and since I was pretty sure Auric didn't have a bionic vibrating dick, I knew it was his phone.

He took a quick peek at it. "It's David."

"And he's wondering where you are." My turn to sigh. "You should go."

I didn't really want him to. Not because I wanted him to protect me, but because I was selfish and wanted him all to myself. Sharing did not come naturally to me. But Auric wasn't the type to allow himself to be stifled.

"Will you be all right?" Auric asked.

Someone choked. "Does this boy not grasp what you're capable of?" Charon sounded incredulous.

"He's funny that way."

He was also very much a tease, seeing as how he plastered his lips to mine, a short-lived kiss, seeing as how his phone buzzed again. A phone that might find itself dropped in a toilet one day. Oops.

With a final quick peck, Auric left, probably off on some mysterious good deed to help rid the world of evil, a quirk of his that drove my dad batty. I thought it was cute.

I unlocked the bar and ushered Charon into Nexus, flicking on the light switches and dispelling the gloom.

"Auric seemed a bit jumpy back there. Did something happen?" Charon seated himself at the bar.

"Bah, nothing major. Just a minor skirmish. I was attacked by a couple of demons yesterday, so now he's gone all overprotective on me."

Charon chuckled. "Give him time,

Muriel. Don't forget, it's not every woman who can confront demons without bursting into tears."

A valid point but still…I was a touch peeved at my sexy lover. A truly smart boyfriend, sensing my horniness when he kissed me at the door, would not have rushed off to meet his buddies for a night of adventuring. No, a true lover would have swept me off my feet and taken me out back for a thorough fuck *then* gone adventuring with his buddies. I wasn't out to cage him from doing the things he felt were important. I just wanted him to do me thoroughly first.

I'd give him a chance to make it up to me later tonight, or heads—and I meant both of them—would roll.

That was hours from now though, and after I was done my shift. I served Charon a mug of frothing Hell brew, not a drink for the uninitiated. I bustled around, work keeping me busy for the remainder of the evening, but when my sister Bambi walked in, I handed over the bar to Percy and beckoned her to follow me out back to my office.

The door shut to keep prying ears from hearing things that might get them killed, I plopped onto the couch I kept in there. My sister perched on my desk, her micro mini skirt riding up and advertising the fact that she wore no panties and had shaved.

I averted my eyes. "Hey, sis, mind crossing your legs? There are some things a girl just doesn't need to see."

Bambi giggled. "Sorry, little lamb, I just got off work. It was a most fulfilling night."

And by fulfilling she meant carnally and esoterically. Bambi was a succubus, which, in a nutshell, meant she had sex with guys and sucked at their life force while doing it. Kind of gross, but I loved her anyway. She'd found the perfect job to keep her fed as a feature exotic dancer, and she did it well, drawing in huge crowds. Apparently she could do things with a pole that defied gravity, kind of like her tits.

"Can I ask you something?" I asked my older and, while perhaps not wiser, more male-experienced sister.

"You can ask me anything, you know that, lamb. What's up?"

"It's about Auric."

"Ooh, a relationship question." Bambi clapped her hands. "I love those. Does your man want you to do something kinky? Tie you up maybe? Spank you?" She recited off a number of naughty things, some which I'd never even heard of but I'd definitely look into for future reference.

"No, it's not about sex." We had no

problems in that department. "It's this whole overprotective crap thing he's got going on. How do I make him understand I can take care of myself?"

"You can't. So you'll have to learn to deal with it." Her serious mien meant she wasn't joking.

I didn't like her answer. "Deal with it? I don't think you understand. He wants me to have someone with me whenever I leave the house just because some demons attacked me. I don't need a babysitter." Said with a petulant jut of my lips that was wasted on my sister.

Bambi rolled her eyes. "Oh, excuse me. How dare he love you so much that he feels a need to keep you safe? What a jerk. I say we kill him."

My cheeks burned as she mocked me. "This isn't funny."

"No, it's sad. You were the one bitching she wanted to wait for the one. For a man who loves me," my sister said in a high falsetto as she clasped at her bosom. "You found him. You got your man, and now you're whining he loves you too much?"

I squirmed in my seat. "Is this your way of telling me to let it slide?"

"Lamb, that man loves you. Totally and utterly. After what happened last month, can you blame him for wanting to be cautious?

And really, what's the big deal?"

Put like that, it made me sound as if I was making a volcano out of vinegar and baking soda. Lots of fizzle, but no real burning inferno.

"So I guess I'm going to have to get used to having a shadow everywhere I go."

"For now. In time, he'll probably ease up more. I mean look, he's no longer sitting in the back corner of the bar glowering at everyone who comes in. Just give it time."

Giving it time meant having patience. I didn't have much of that. But I did have manners—just to piss my dad off. "Thanks, sis."

"Anytime, lamb. Now if you don't mind, I'm going to go bust a move because I hear my favorite song playing." She hopped off my desk and opened my office door. Out she sashayed to the musical beat of Salt-N-Pepa's, 'Push It'.

Gotta love the '80s.

As the bar was shutting down, David, Auric's best friend, walked in. If I hadn't been so in love with Auric, I might have admired— for longer and with lustier thoughts—the way his shaggy blond hair always fell in a tousled mess around his vividly blue eyes. I might have noticed the way his white T-shirt hugged the slim, muscled physique of his upper body and the way his lean waist and long legs filled out the tight-fitting jeans he wore nicely. Since I was in a committed relationship, I only barely noticed those types of things anymore. Damn, I was becoming an awesome liar, even to myself.

"Hey, David," I called out. "Where's Auric?"

"He and Christopher got hung up, so they sent me to walk you home."

I rolled my eyes. "They do realize I'm a grown woman, right?"

"I'm just doing what they asked me." He held his hands up in surrender.

David was such a pussy cat; literally. He might seem shy and boyish, but that lasted only until he shapeshifted into a blond panther of incredible agility and strength. Once that happened, watch out, because kitty had claws.

"You can tell them you tried. Go home and get some sleep. Or, even better, find yourself a hot little thing and get laid." Being blissfully happy and sexually sated most of the time, I now believed everyone should enjoy the same state.

Poor David, that type of talk made him shift uncomfortably. "I don't know any girls. And besides, I can't leave. I said I would walk you home, and Auric will freak if I don't."

"David, David, David," I chided. "You and I both know you can't make me do anything."

"Auric said you'd say that, and he told me to tell you, um—" David blushed, a trait about him that I found superbly cute, given his deadly shapeshifter alter ego. "He's the man in this relationship, and if he says you need an escort to walk you home that you'd better listen, or you will be punished."

I laughed. Didn't Auric know by now I looked forward to his punishments? The last time he'd made me scream for hours on end, and when I'd come, I'd coasted on the power high for days afterward, not to mention I'd orgasmed so copiously we'd had to change the sheets.

"Tell you what, I'll let you walk me home if you promise to tell him just how bad I was about it."

Confusion creased his features.

I sighed and spelled it out for him. "I want him to punish me, David. I really, *really* like it when he does, if you know what I mean." My wink probably wasn't necessary, but it was fun because David's cheeks turned an even ruddier color.

I laughed and thought that would end it.

With more backbone than I would have assumed, David blurted out. "He said if you didn't listen, he wouldn't let you play with him tonight and he'd play with himself in front of you instead."

I gaped at David. I couldn't believe Auric had threatened that, let alone that David had repeated it.

"Do you like to watch?" asked David, meeting my eyes briefly before ducking his head again while I still stood there tongue-tied.

His question surprised me, as did the flushed look on his face. Peering unobtrusively down, I could see his face wasn't the only thing flushing with blood. "I—um." I was at a loss for words. How shocking, me, embarrassed. It seemed strange, but I had reason. While I didn't mind flirting and tossing out the sexual innuendoes and jokes, it seemed a little wrong to do so when David so obviously found it titillating. "You'll have to ask Auric," was my prim reply, but even as I said that, I had an image of David watching me and Auric fucking while he stroked himself. I didn't need my wet panties to know how much I'd enjoy it.

But I was in a committed, *monogamous* relationship. No voyeurs allowed. No threesomes. No orgies.

Odd, but I couldn't help a smidgen of disappointment. Which, in turn, made me feel guilty. Which, in turn, irritated me. As a princess of Hell, I should never feel guilty but rejoice in the fact I had sinful thoughts.

And that was all they were. Thoughts. Feelings. I wouldn't act on them. Fantasy was allowed.

With all the patrons gone, I put away the cash and receipts for the day before locking the bar. As I headed back to the loft I shared with Auric, David walked beside me, hands stuffed in his pockets, gaze fixed on the ground.

"The concrete sidewalk is looking especially fine tonight," I teased.

"Sorry." He shot me a quick look, and I blew him a kiss. Back down went his head.

I stifled a giggle. His shy demeanor and easy blushes brought out my devilish side—blame my father. It was his DNA that made me do it. Being naturally bad, I couldn't help myself, I had to ask. "David, do you like to watch people having sex?"

No peeking at me this time. He just nodded and pretended a great interest in his moving feet.

"Have you ever watched Auric doing it?" It didn't seem like the type of thing Auric would be into, but then again, you never knew. He and David were pretty close.

I could see David's cheeks pinken, and again he nodded. I admit I found this concept highly titillating. A voyeur, damn that made me wetter, not that I was looking for an audience—yet.

"Did Auric know you were watching?" Apparently I'd have to wait for that answer, as David heard the whisper of sound a second before I did, and we both smelled the sulfuric tang of Hell. Demon time.

While I yanked knives from sheaths, David's body rippled, his clothes shredding from his lanky frame as the kitty nestled inside him burst free. Gross, yet, at the same time, kind of hot. His animal shape had a power and grace that was attractive.

Silver daggers in hand, I prepared to invoke the magic that would cause them to burn with Hellfire.

A guttural chuckle sounded from the depths of a dark alley, and David, now a hulking golden panther spun to face it with a snarl. His muzzle drew back over very large incisors.

I snarled myself when I saw who hid in the shadows. "Azazel! You cowardly slug. Why can't you come at me in the open instead of hiding? Then again, with a face like yours, I'd hide, too."

"Lucifer's daughter," spat back the large black demon as he stepped into view. "Such a saucy mouth. Not for long. Soon, you'll be screaming my name when I make you my concubine."

Before he'd turned traitor, Azazel had been one of my father's most trusted commanders, and he'd also fancied himself my suitor. Only one problem—I never could stand him. Apparently he still had fantasies about me though, fantasies that would get him castrated if he didn't leave me alone.

"Get yourself a pocket pussy if you're that hard up." Yeah, I knew I was inciting the whole tail-pulling thing. What could I say? I thrived on danger.

"Bitch, you'll rue your words when you are mine."

"Bring it on, little man, and I mean little." I taunted him some more.

Incensed, Azazel roared. His black eyes glowed with fury, and his fangs dripped a mixture of venom and drool.

But my father was Satan. I'd grown up with a hell of a lot worse, so I yawned. "Do you mind hurrying this up? I've got a leftover pizza at home with my name on it."

Azazel lowered his voice menacingly. "My master"—I pretended I didn't feel myself flinch at the word—"is looking forward to seeing you. He said to tell you, when winter arrives, he'll be waiting for you by the furnace."

I blinked. "Say what? What the hell is it with you bad guys and your cryptic messages? Did it never occur to you that you should give me, like, an actual date and time? I mean, what if I've got a hair appointment scheduled that day or a tanning session? Christmas is coming and I'll be pissed if you cut into those festivities. And how come you get to pick the location? You guys chose it last time. I think it should my turn this time," I babbled trying to fight the panic that kept trying to push itself up past my gorge.

*Don't let the master come back. Don't let the master touch me.*

A part of me knew, if I let myself think too much about Azazel's threat, I'd start screaming. "You know what? You tell that piece-of-shit coward the next time he wants to talk to me, he can make a fucking appointment. I'm through playing your fucking games. David, eat the giant rat."

With a growl, which I swear sounded happy, David pounced, knocking a surprised Azazel to the ground. The big demon unfortunately possessed superior strength, though, and sent my kitty flying. Eight lives left.

"You'll pay for that, Satan's child," Azazel threatened. A curse marred by the blood dripping down his face.

I stuck my tongue out at him. "Na-na-na-na-boo-boo."

Why act mature when childish antics were more fun?

A claw was swiped in my direction, but in his rage, Azazel was clumsy, and I sliced a talon-tipped finger off.

The severed limb twitched on the ground. I let my teeth show in a wicked smile, and I was sure the flames of Hell lit my eyes. I looked totally badass, badass enough that Azazel took a step back.

"You'll pay for that."

"I'll pay?" I smirked. "No, you will for thinking you could betray my dad and for attacking my boyfriend. Way I see it, you owe me your life."

But Azazel wasn't one to pay his debts. As David came bounding back, recovered from his impromptu flight, Azazel called a portal and jumped through. What a surprise. Azazel was a bigger pussy than David.

Poor David looked upset that his cat toy had gotten away.

"Good kitty." I rubbed David's big furry head behind the ears, an action that was rewarded with purring on the sound level of an aircraft carrier taking off. "I thought big cats couldn't purr?" I could have sworn I'd seen a documentary on it, but then again,

David was no ordinary feline. "Come on, let's get back to my place so we can find you some clothes." I somehow doubted the remnants littering the ground would cover any important parts, and I knew I was too curious to look away. Shapeshifters must have one hell of a clothing budget, on par with the Hulk's.

They also had, for the most part, fit bods that tempted a girl, and being a tad hungry, I didn't want to give in to temptation.

Even if it would taste good.

# CHAPTER FIVE

Auric walked in about ten seconds after David went into the bathroom to change. My nose twitched. I smelled brimstone, and despite my encounter with Azazel, it wasn't coming from me. A peek behind Auric showed my father didn't accompany him. I crossed my arms and looked at him coolly.

"And just where have you been?" I tapped my foot. I already knew. I just wanted to see what he'd answer.

His lips twitched. "You do realize you're the image of the irate housewife?"

"Try more like psychotic girlfriend."

"I don't suppose there's any point in lying?"

"Only if you're trying to curtail favor with my dad. So, what's the deal?"

"The deal is I guess I should have taken a shower before coming home."

"Yes, because a man who leaves on a mysterious mission returning smelling of soap isn't suspicious at all." I rolled my eyes. "Now that you're no longer an angel, you're going to have to really work on your subterfuge."

"Or disarm you with honesty." His smile

was designed to melt my panties. It did, but it didn't melt my need to know what was going on.

"You want to play the honesty game, then let's start. What were you doing in Hell?" I left out the "without me." It peeved me off that my lover's first visit to the pit hadn't been by my side. I'd meticulously planned how I would flaunt my super-hot boyfriend when I finally convinced him to go to Hell.

"I had stuff to take care of." He didn't even have the decency to look abashed at his vague answer.

"Stuff!" I stalked toward him and poked him in the chest with one finger, making him flinch. Don't scoff. I gave a mean poke. "Don't you start with the oblique answers, buddy. I want the truth." Which would totally peeve my dad, who said truth was for the unimaginative.

"Your dad wanted to talk to me, so I paid him a visit."

My jaw dropped. That hadn't been the answer I expected, especially since Auric was still alive after a meeting with Daddy dear. What did my father want with Auric? "Was my dad trying to bribe you into leaving me?"

"No."

"Did he attempt to kill you?" Which would totally piss me off. I didn't like people, even a well-meaning father, threatening those I loved.

"Nope."

Irritated by his short replies, steam might have come from my ears, I definitely had a bit of fire in my growled, "So what did he want then?"

"He wanted to talk."

"Since when are you and the devil bosom buddies?"

My words made him cringe, and he replied with a stiff, "We're not friends, but we do have one thing in common—you."

Great, the two most important men in my life were talking behind my back. I hated secrets, unless I was in the loop. Then they were tons of fun.

"What did my father want?" Other than an end to world peace, more gravy with his steak, and a statue of him in that famous wax museum. When I pointed out people liked to grope and do obscene things with those statues and take pictures, he'd grinned and said, "Exactly." But I somehow doubted he and Auric had discussed any of this.

*They were talking about me.*

"Your dad is worried about you, Muriel. He's not the only one."

Spin the broken record. "I'm fine." Dandy. Just fucking peachy keen.

I moved away from Auric and, with nothing better to do with my hands, tidied up. I wasn't about to have another talk about my nightmares, and I most certainly didn't want to tell him about yet another demon appearance. Auric would lose his ever-loving mind—and temper. Which, in retrospect, was kind of hot.

However, talking about the nightmares and stuff? Not so much.

"No, you're not fine." Auric followed me and placed his hands over mine to still them. "You wake up screaming every night. You flinch whenever you see someone in a hooded robe or if someone says the word 'master'."

As if to give him even more ammo, I flinched and immediately wanted to slug him in the gut for being right. "I have issues. I'll get over them."

"It's more than issues, baby. You're scared, dammit. Terrified. Why can't you just admit it?"

"Am not," I retorted out of habit. "I'm not scared of anything." My dad probably beamed in pride as I lied through my teeth.

"And that's why your dad wanted to talk to me. He thinks, and I happen to agree with him, there might be something more going on here than we can see. Something that's making you so scared."

Gee, wasn't being tortured by some

magical asshat in a robe enough? Shudder. Why was it I could confront demons and mouth off, but think of a robed asshole too cowardly to show his face and I wanted to collapse to the floor in a shivering heap? Maybe Auric had a point. Not that I would tell him. Never let a man know he was right, something they taught me in Keeping a Man on His Toes 304.

"I don't understand what's going on." Truly, I didn't. At times I wondered if perhaps I should have been born a blonde. Apparently they had more fun, and I could use some of that right about now.

"I'm not sure what's happening either."

I shot a sharp look his way. "But you suspect something?"

"Yeah. Maybe. I don't want to say anything until I know for sure. But, both your dad and I think you should meet with some of his mages."

"Why, so they can hypnotize me and make me dance like a chicken whenever I hear the word"—I swallowed hard—"m-master?"

"First off, I would never let them do that."

"And if they tried?"

"I'd kill them."

I uttered a happy sigh. I loved it when he got all implacable. So sexy. "I don't know what you expect them to find. Last I heard dreams come from the subconscious, and my cowardly streak where you-know-who is concerned is a mental issue. And before you suggest"—because my dad had—"I am not open to either electric shock therapy or a lobotomy."

"That's just it, baby. I don't think this problem is natural. I don't think you have a mental issue at all, which is why I want someone on his magical team to have a look at you."

I might have replied, but right at that moment, a new player entered the conversation.

"Thanks for the clothes…" David came out of the bathroom and stopped talking as Auric swung a glower his way.

Uh-oh.

"Why did David need clothes?" Auric asked tightly.

Tell him the truth and have him freak or… "I tore the clothes right off him in a fit of insane lust." I smiled.

A normal guy might have snapped right about now and either yelled at me or tried to kill his friend. Auric laughed. "Sure you did."

He didn't believe me? Was he calling me a liar? I stamped my foot. "I did so have wild sex with him."

"It's not what you think," David interjected, his hands spread wider than his eyes.

"I know exactly what to think. You got attacked on the way home."

A frowned creased my brow. "Were you spying on me?"

"No. But why else would David need clothes?"

"I told you because I ripped them clean from his body."

I was less than impressed with Auric's snort. "Please, as if I'd seriously believe for a moment you and David had messed around?" Auric laughed, which made me frown at him. I mean I was happy and all he trusted me, but still, a little jealousy would have been nice. Had the roles been reversed, I'd have had the other woman in a choke hold and pulled out most of her hair by now.

His continued mirth annoyed me. I knew just the thing to wipe the smile from his face. "You want the truth? David had to go furry because Azazel paid me a visit on my way home."

That sobered him quickly. Auric's face darkened, and his lip curled. "What did that spawn of evil want?"

"He wanted to tell me that…that…" I froze, and the words stuck in my throat. I couldn't tell Auric that Azazel claimed that robed one was coming for me. I didn't even want to think it.

But my lover figured it out, probably because the panic that had threatened me earlier enveloped me and I fell to my knees, wheezing. Lucky me, I didn't face plant as several pairs of arms wrapped around me. Apparently both David and Auric caught me before I fell.

A shame their comforting embrace didn't stop the damned shivers.

"What happened?" Auric's query emerged in a tight voice. He gathered me onto his lap and plopped onto the couch. I huddled in the cradling circle of his arms.

David answered for me on account of I still had trouble breathing. Maybe I had allergies? *Yeah, an allergy that only spilled blood will cure.*

"Azazel said something about his master waiting for her when winter hit around the furnace. Honestly, it didn't make much sense. Muriel then sliced a piece of him off, and the demon went back to Hell."

"He didn't stay to fight?"

Regaining some of my wits—not all of them because sanity was overrated—I finally managed to say something. "Of course he didn't stay to fight. Azazel knows I can kick his ass."

"Or he wants you alive."

Auric didn't have to say "for something worse." It was implied.

"Whether he wants me dead or alive, his message didn't make sense. I mean, come on, he mumbled something about when winter hits blah, blah, blah, and something about a furnace. All I got to say is they better not be planning mischief around Christmas. I've got plans." No one ruined my holidays.

"You celebrate the birth of Christ?" asked David, his brows high in surprise.

"Not exactly. As you well know, Jesus wasn't born in December. Nope, we celebrate the winter solstice by decorating a big-ass tree, setting it on fire, and dancing naked around it."

I said this so seriously that it took David a minute to realize I was messing with him.

"You do not," he exclaimed.

I cracked up at the look in his face. "Oh, please. Of course I celebrate Christmas. Like hello, lots of presents for me. Did you really think I'd skip a holiday like that?"

"But your dad is Satan…" Poor David was still puzzled.

"Yes, and is there anything more twisted than the world's current version of Christmas? My dad loves the holidays. He gets totally drunk off the greed and avarice. Not to mention all the fornicating that happens at office parties. It's his favorite time of the year."

"That's just sick," said David with disgust.

I couldn't help it. I giggled.

"Be nice," Auric murmured in my ear. "David still has delusions when it comes to his concept of Heaven and Hell."

"Apparently."

One good thing? Our inane conversation had helped calm me down. This whole panic thing was really starting to piss me off. At my core, I knew I didn't fear. I just wish my body would listen.

I wanted to be in control again.

"Auric?" I said softly.

"Yeah, baby?" He stroked my hair.

"I want to see those mages." Me, relenting? And so quickly? I wasn't an idiot. I could kick, fight and scream about it for a few weeks, but the truth remained, something was wrong with me. These increasing panic attacks weren't normal, and I wanted them gone. If it took letting some freaky demon headshrinker fix it, then shrink away. Unless they went near my booty or boobs. Try to reduce their size and someone would die.

"You say when and we'll go."

I loved this man whose world revolved around me. "Now," I said before I changed my mind, not to mention I wanted the brave me back, not this frightened little wimp that I wanted to slap silly.

"Can I come?" asked David.

"Muriel?"

Why not? "Sure. Come one, come all, and see the sights of Hell. Let me get changed first, though. If I'm going for a visit, then I need to look the part." As a princess of Hell, a certain amount of pizzazz was expected. I didn't want to let the damned down.

I made the boys turn their backs—well, David anyway, but I wondered if there was reflective surface giving him a peek. Just in case, I made sure I did everything with sensual grace and succeeded if the smoldering interest in Auric's gaze was any indication.

As to what I wore? A short leather skirt with a black lace thong underneath. A lace-up corset that gave me cleavage that would swallow a hand whole. Over-the-knee, zipped leather boots with stilettos that could do serious damage. Eyes outlined in black, bright red lipstick, and a crackling brush of my long hair and I looked vampy enough for a visit.

Appreciation glowed in Auric's eyes, the bright green, which reminded me of spring, a sign of his lust. David's bright blue eyes were equally appreciative when I twirled for them. Some days I loved being a girl. Some? Ha. I always loved being a girl. And I totally dug being the center of attention.

Modesty wasn't something I subscribed to.

I let Auric open the portal to Hell. Why not? Ever since my dad gave him his shadowy wings and access to magic, my man could do all manner of things—some of them without hands to my erotic delight. I could have opened a rift to my home. However, I preferred to save my energy for a 'just in case'.

Unlike some pansy group of adventurers, we didn't hold hands. Fuck that. I was a princess. Head held high, I led the way, and the boys followed.

As soon as I stepped through, an act that took only a single heartbeat, which sent a deep chill pinging through me, I felt the difference.

Heat was the first sensation, a sharp, dry heat given we were leagues away from the Styx. On top of the warmth, there was the ash, a light dust that coated everything and filled the lungs yet didn't choke—unless you were a newbie like David, who gasped as he beheld the underworld for the first time. The poor guy went into a coughing fit.

As Auric pounded him on the back, I took a peek around.

The real world had gotten some facts about Hell right over the years. Yes, the underworld was hot, noisy, and there was a constant ash sifting down from the grayish sky. But that was where the bible version of Hell and reality stopped.

There were no damned chained to rocks while being whipped. No demons torturing souls strung by their heels. At least not in public.

What the nine circles of Hell did have was a lot of ramshackle housing and people. Billions upon billions living much like they had above, but without the green grass and white picket fences. Wrought iron was the yard boundary of choice.

One thing we thankfully didn't have down here was cars. The smog would have proved untenable. However, the lack of motorized transportation made getting where you wanted to go in a hurry a bit of a pain, like now.

People crowded the road to my dad's palace, impeding our progress. They were watching some kind of protester on a soapbox causing havoc.

Did this street prophet not realize I'd arrived and had places to go? Out of my way. Awesome princess coming.

Alas, I didn't shout to announce my

arrival. No need to pinpoint my location for assassins, that and I was kind of miffed no one noticed my exalted presence.

Sure it would have been easier to teleport within the palace itself, but Dad leaned toward paranoia and had a magical shield created against that sort of thing within the palace and the area just surrounding it.

Tension and alertness made my lover stiff—as opposed to stiff from desire. Auric wrapped an arm around my waist, so deliciously possessive, and tucked me tight to his side. At a nod from Auric, David glued himself to my other side.

Oh yummy, a sandwich, just not a very fun one. At least in the books, when a girl got sandwiched, everybody was naked. Now there was a mental image to make me blush—and flush in interesting places.

Somewhat distracted by the male bodies brushing me on either side didn't mean I forgot to protest. "There's no need for this. I'm a princess down here, remember?" Something the crowds they bulldozed through didn't seem to be recognizing, to my annoyance. I hadn't been gone that long.

"I am your consort, and as such, I am officially appointing David as your bodyguard. Which means we're not budging. So smile for the people, and let's get out of here. I don't like the size of this crowd. It's too easy for someone to sneak up on us."

I'd stopped listening pretty much at consort. Who had appointed Auric my consort? And did I care?

I knew Auric was my soul mate. This decision to appoint himself my consort—giggle—just confirmed he felt the same way. As for my newly designated bodyguard, judging by the way his body pressed against mine, I guess he planned to protect me by using himself as a shield. He certainly felt hard enough to block any blows.

The guys edged me around the commotion. In other words, Auric and David manhandled people out of the way. Some might have argued, but funny how a few intense glowers and well-aimed fists got the point across. The crowd moved enough for me to see what had them so riveted.

A demon, not quite a minor league player given his size, but nothing close to a major seeing as how he had only medium-sized horns, stood on a rock, preaching.

"...is coming. The one true leader shall end the travesty that is Heaven and Hell. Death shall become meaningless. The barriers shall be torn down and God and Satan destroyed."

I couldn't stifle a gasp. What blasphemy

was this? How dared a minion of Hell preach against not just my father but my uncle, too? And why wasn't anyone stopping him?

Pulling free from my lover, I stood straight and shouted. "Shut the fuck up." Eloquent? Maybe not, but effective. It drew eyes to me, eyes that Auric and David countered with ferocious scowls as they flanked me.

It also drew the attention of the demon on the soapbox—in this case actually one for blood oranges. "If it isn't Hell's whore herself."

How rude.

# CHAPTER SIX

Some insults I took with pride. Some I insisted on, but one thing I usually didn't do was take credit for things I wasn't and that belonged to others. "I think you have me mistaken with my sister, Bambi. I'm Muriel."

A murmur went through the crowd along with several shrugs and whispers of, "Who?"

I rolled my eyes. "I am Satana Muriel Baphomet. The other infamous daughter."

I heard "ah's" of understanding and even more stroking to my ego, "She's the one who killed all those demons by the abyss," followed by a deflating, "Her fault we had to work overtime cleaning it up."

Whiners. See if I saved them if another apocalypse struck.

Okay, I would, but only so I could bask in their thanks and adulation. I didn't do shit for free.

"Thou art the progeny of all that is wrong with this plane."

"My dad isn't the problem. If you have a problem with how Hell is run, then move on. The abyss is waiting."

Not exactly a politically correct answer,

but I had no patience for those who claimed they could do better. Hell wasn't a place where the good and kind came. Well, some did, but it should be kept in mind that every damned soul in this place had sinned. Big sin or little sin, it didn't matter. They were the purveyors of their own demise. And if they didn't like it, then they could move out.

As to the demons, well, suck it up. This was their world, and even I knew they needed a strong hand to keep them in line. Left unattended, the demonic hordes would quickly tear each other apart in power bids.

The problem with my words and beliefs was they were true. And no one liked painful truth. The crowd murmured, and expressions took on ugly casts, abetted by the ranting demon who pointed at me and said, "A blow against her is a blow against the dictatorship of her father."

The crowd around us began to move closer, undeterred by Auric and David. While I'd dressed for the visit, and had my knives, I'd neglected to bring along my sword. Auric had his, and he loosened it while David rolled his shoulders and his body tensed, the beast lurking just under his skin.

I placed a hand on each of their arms to stall them. Their intervention would not be required. I could see the black horns and towering wing tips of my father's demonic guard moving in. The best of the best. I spotted Remy in the group, a rascally fire demon who often laughed as he fought. Xaphan, always so serious. And many more that I'd met over the years.

They dove on the preaching demon, no weapons needed, not with so many fists aimed the rabble-rouser's way. With a firm grip, my father's demonic force dragged him away, more than likely to face a few hundred years of torture for his words, words he could not stop spouting.

"Soon shall ye see the truth of my words. The true master is coming. You shall note the master's arrival, as the flames of Hell shall be extinguished. You will see. You—"

At the word master, I couldn't help but shiver, a chill possessing me even in the midst of this stifling heat, and even the hot press of the guys on either side couldn't melt it.

Surely the mutiny-minded demon couldn't be speaking of the same master, the one I dreamed of nightly? Yet his words…something about them rang true.

My overactive mind couldn't help conjuring images of the master returning. Finding me and cornering me. Hurting me.

Sob.

My knees would have buckled had the

boys not held me upright, almost dragging me through the murmuring crowd. Snippets of conversations came to me.

"Bah, Satan's not that bad."

"If death is abolished, can I go back to my house? I miss my dog."

"That princess is fucking hot!"

I managed a quick wave at the person who complimented me, a quick wave because, with grim faces, the boys still carried me along like a piece of luggage, a hot and nicely dressed one.

With the soapbox talker gone now, a few of the damned finally deigned to celebrate my presence. I could hear them murmuring. "Satana" ... "It's the princess" ... "Slut!"

I might have taken offence at the last, but I could hear the jealousy in the female tone. And really, how could I blame her? I had the two hottest guys in Hades glued to my side. Oh, if only my succubus sisters could see me know. They'd be high-fiving their little sister for scoring.

When we cleared the crowd, we made much better time, briskly walking to the gates of the palace. No guards stood at their opening, and for those that wondered, they gaped open at all times because no one was stupid enough to try and get my father's attention on purpose.

Although Daddy kept hoping. He did enjoy a bit of sport.

As we stepped into the courtyard of my father's castle slash mansion slash huge freaking monstrosity, the guys finally relaxed a bit. David peeled away from my side and moved behind us as a rear guard while Auric dropped his possessive arm from around my waist and clasped my hand instead. Strangely, I felt disappointment. I'd kind of enjoyed their dual close proximity. Not that I would think of cheating on Auric, but a girl was allowed to fantasize, right?

As we walked up the palace steps, the mighty black doors to the palace swung open with a nasty creak—totally intentional—and out scurried the squat form of my father's major domo. A cross between a gremlin and an Atlantian—a pairing that boggled the mind—the odd creature ran my father's palace with frightening efficiency. Essentially, you toed the line, or you ended up on latrine detail for eternity.

"Polkie," I exclaimed, rushing forward, dragging Auric, who wouldn't let my hand go, with me. I hugged my old friend one-armed and kissed the top of his bald, scaly head.

Polkie, more formally known as Philokrates, split his lips in what passed for smile. "Satana," he said with obvious pleasure, which made me feel kind of guilty. I hadn't visited home in a while. With Dad popping in constantly to check up on me, I'd forgotten that there were other people who might miss me. "Your father will be so happy you've come to visit. I see you've brought your consort and guard."

What? Did everyone know about my consort before I did? Another thing for Auric and me to talk about later.

"Is Dad around?" I asked, striding into the palace, my heeled boots clacking nicely on the slate floor.

"Yes, he's in the throne room, passing judgment."

"Don't tell him we're coming. I want to surprise him." I dragged my consort—I'd have to be careful not to giggle when I said it out loud—and, with David following, took them through a maze of corridors until we reached the throne room where my father held court.

In somewhat medieval fashion, my father sat on a mighty throne and judged the damned that had truly been evil in life. Everybody else—the white liars, the petty criminals—got their judgment from a book of preset punishments. It made things simpler and tended to reduce the number of complaints about preferential treatment. It also meant that Dad had more free time to pursue other things—like short skirts.

We sneaked into the throne room and stood with a crowd of damned at the back. There was a long line of people leading to the witness box, waiting for their turn to point the finger of blame at the accused, a portly, bald fellow who smiled smugly, still proud of his crimes for the moment.

As a damned one sobbed out her story, my father suddenly stood. He roared. "Silence." As usual, he got what he wanted. "To the accused," and, no, my dad didn't name him because to name him was to admit he knew him. My father preferred to treat the worst of the worst as nonentities. Not even minor blips on his sinful radar. "The crimes against you are numerous. Drug trafficking, assassination, lying, cheating, but the nastiest thing you ever did, by far the most despicable even by my standards, was your kidnapping of young girls and selling them as sex slaves."

I, and the rest of the crowd, grumbled in anger—heinous indeed. But I knew Dad wouldn't let us down.

"I sentence thee…" Daddy dear paused for effect. "To be drawn and quartered daily for the next five hundred years and to serve as a whore for Hell's army."

The accused finally lost his smile and stood in a panic. "You can't do that. I should be rewarded for being evil. It got me here."

My father smiled, not a pretty sight for the uninitiated. "Welcome to Hell. I've just fucked you like you fucked over thousands. Enjoy your stay."

Kicking and screaming, the scuzzbag was dragged away to the cheers of the crowd.

Do the crime, do the time. That was my father's motto. Hell wasn't a reward for those who did evil; it was the punishment. And those who enjoyed their crimes in their previous life, let's just say they were made to regret it over and over and…

The damned souls dispersed, many smiling, others sobbing, happy to see justice at last.

I approached my father, who bounded off his throne and gave me a hug, which was so totally out of character I almost screamed in fright.

"What the fuck, Dad?" I finally managed to say.

"What? Can't a father be glad his daughter's come home for a visit?"

I eyed him suspiciously, but my dad just smiled benignly back. I didn't like it. Something had to be seriously wrong for my dad to be worried enough to hug me in public.

"Other fathers maybe, but you should be asking me if I'm back to lead an uprising and take my rightful spot as heir."

Daddy laughed. "Oh, please. You hate politics and paperwork even more than I do."

I did. "I need your help." It galled me to ask, but the direct approach, in this case, was the best tactic. I would just have to remember not to sign anything or make any promises. Daddy did so love to collect souls, even from his children.

"I take it Auric spoke to you about our suspicions," said my father.

"Yeah. You guys think maybe the stranger put some kind of spell on me." I only quivered a little using such an abstract term.

My shiver didn't go unnoticed. A frown drew my father's formidable brows together. "Don't fear, daughter. We will remove this curse from you and free you to once again be a bloodthirsty pox upon the world."

"Ah, Daddy, you say the nicest things." While I understood the affection in his words, I couldn't help but giggle when I saw David's slack-jawed face. "What's wrong?"

"N-nothing," David stammered.

Daddy bulked himself to loom over the cat shifter. "Tell anyone about my mental lapse and show of affection and you will make a great rug in my office."

"Yes, sir. I mean, no, sir. I mean—"

Auric snorted. "He's fucking with you,

David. He won't lay a hand on you unless you betray him or his daughter."

"If you're done showing off, pissing words, then do you mind? I'd like to get this over with." Patience, especially this close to our goal, just wasn't happening.

With Daddy leading the way, we went to meet with Hades' finest minds, the ones who still had one at any rate.

As we wandered and I chatted with Daddy about things, David lost some of his anxiety. He even loosened up enough to venture a question. "How big is this place?" David stared around with obvious amazement at the vast arched rooms and colorfully painted frescoes we passed.

"As big as I need it," boasted my father. Eager to show off—because he did so like inciting envy—Daddy started pointing out things. "See that painting over there?" The image in question was of a satyr licking his lips as he watched maidens bathe in a secluded glen. A masterpiece, beautifully rendered, down to the individual strands of hair. "That was done by Michelangelo. What a coup getting him was! My brother, God, is still pissed over losing him."

As my dad regaled David with stories, it made me think of the memories I had of growing up here. Happy memories, actually, even though I'd done my best to drive my dad nuts.

Like the time I'd painted his throne room pink because I thought it would look pretty. That he might have tolerated, but the big smiley faces and flowers I'd added as a finishing touch had pushed him over the edge.

During my school days as a straight A student—my brain had been much sharper back then—my father had often lamented about the fact that I studied and applied myself. When I'd complained some of my succubi sisters had straight As, too, he'd informed me they did it the traditional way— by sleeping with their teachers and blackmailing them.

Not liking his answer, and being stubborn, I'd responded to it in the only way possible. I'd gotten a scholarship. Wow, did the shit hit the fan when that honor came through. The steam had literally poured from his ears.

Then there had been the whole I'm-staying-a-virgin-until-I-fall-in-love thing. I'd stuck to my guns on that one no matter how many gifts my father tried to bribe me with.

Ah, the good old days. Now I could do no wrong. I owned a bar and helped people get drunk and lose their inhibitions. I lived in sin with a fallen angel. And I carried a balance on my credit cards. What could I say? All those years rebelling and I ended up turning into a model daughter after all.

One of my father's demon aides came loping up and handed him a missive. My father opened it and scowled. "Damn my brother. We lost him."

"Him who?" I asked.

"That kid artist I was keeping my eye on."

Suddenly I knew who he spoke of. Jimmy Santos. A gifted artist, only sixteen and whose soul my father had been actively working on.

David leaned over and whispered in my ear. "Why is Satan so upset? I mean he's got billions of souls, so why care if he loses one?"

"My dad takes his work very seriously. This one soul he lost, the kid was a fantastic artist. We're talking some serious skill here. His paintings could move you to tears. And Heaven got him."

"I thought that was a good thing."

"Did Auric not explain anything about Heaven to you?" Once the secret of Auric being an angel came out, I'd asked Auric about Heaven. He explained it to me, and my dad confirmed it. In a nutshell, "Heaven is a place that never changes. A place of perfect and endless summer days."

"And what's wrong with that?"

"Imagine, if you will, the perfect piece of toast. How do you know it's perfect?"

"Because it's not burnt."

"But if your toast is the same every single day, how long before you stop appreciating it and it turns bland? Boring? Now back to the artist. He's gone to Heaven. His paintings that could evoke such feeling? That's over and done. That boy will never paint a masterpiece again, one, because Heaven doesn't like change and, two, because having nothing to suffer, he'll lose that depth of emotion. So much talent and all lost because my dad couldn't get him to commit even one small sin."

"That's messed up," said David, his face thoughtful.

It was, but it was how it worked and had since the planes came into existence and the rules were set out. As to who created those rules? Even my dad couldn't answer that one.

The path we took went from richly appointed rooms and corridors to a dank hallway, narrow, the stone rough. Shadows tried to cling to our skin, and the closed space muffled sound and pressed upon our spirits.

In silence now, we continued on our way until we reached a dark archway inscribed with warnings that kept all but the bravest from entering. I didn't bother reading or translating the inscription to the boys. Some things didn't need to be spoken aloud.

A twining set of stone steps led us deep into the bowels of the palace. Smoky torches lit our way, their flickering light creating rather than dissipating shadows, and I could have sworn I saw more than one dark shape scurry away. Good thing David had a firm grip on his kitty, although I would have probably laughed my ass off if he'd turned all furry and chased after the rodents that lived down here. Especially since most of them were larger than expected and bloodthirsty.

Finally, we arrived. About time, too, since my heels had been made to look hot, not actually walk great distances.

Welcome to Frankenstein's lair, or at least my visual idea of it. Wooden tables teemed with beakers. Glass tubing spun in loops while colorful potions smoked noxiously. The shelves lining the dark stone walls sagged under the weight of jars, hundreds of them in all kinds of sizes and shapes. The ones with clear glass made even my iron stomach protest as genetic anomalies and creatures—in some cases only parts of—floated in liquids.

The place spooked me, and to think, the two most important men in my life wanted me to let the owners of said items poke around in my head. If I went home with any body parts missing, there would be Hell to pay. And it wouldn't be cheap.

Shuffling steps signaled we weren't alone, and I watched as three wizened creatures—they might have been human once, it was hard to tell—came forward to meet us.

"I've brought her. Now fix her," said my father without any preamble.

Gotta love him.

I figured they'd be poking and prodding at me for hours. To my surprise it took only fifteen minutes, and to my relief, it didn't involve any of the jars. They simply placed their hands—talk about dry and in need of hand cream—on my head. Other than chapped skin, I didn't feel a darned thing.

Auric held my hand as I stood there trying not to fidget. As if by some unseen signal, they all removed their hands at once, and they went off in a huddle whispering, which, as anyone who knew me would tell you, annoyed the fuck out of me.

Oops, there was that word again. Fuck. Ever since meeting Auric, it had begun dominating more and more of my thoughts and spoken vocabulary. It had a certain elegance to it that I liked. Who the fuck cared? Argh. This was how I knew I was nervous. I babbled inside my own mind.

Finally, the Alzheimer candidate huddle

broke, and with Auric's arms wrapped around me—probably more for the mages' protection than mine in case I didn't like what they had to say—they approached me.

The shortest of them, its face so wrinkled you couldn't tell whether it was male or female, spoke for the group. "Lucifer's daughter, you do indeed have many geas placed upon you."

Duh! "I know that," I snapped. Nervous, I didn't even try to temper my tone or words.

"Most are old and powerful beyond our ken, but there is one that is much more recent. After examining it, we believe it has only one purpose. To frighten and control you."

Again, duh! "So how do we remove it?"

"Only you can do so. Think of it as a magical parasite on the part of your mind that controls memory and bravery. When your memory of this so-called master is triggered." I flinched. "Then so is your fear. To remove the magical parasite, you need to blast it with stronger magic."

"So do it."

The raisin lady snorted. "It is not something an outside force can do. You must increase your stores of magic and, in doing so, will free yourself."

"Where and how do I get stronger magic?" Ooh, maybe I'd have to go on a quest and find a lost magical artifact.

"There is no where. As to how, your magic is sexually based?" the wizened one asked. I nodded, trying not to blush. It still bothered me. "Then you need to have more sex," it said bluntly.

Now we were talking. "Hear that, babe?" I tilted my head back and smiled at Auric. "We're gonna have to increase our sexual intake. Prepare for a marathon."

"No," interjected the crone. "You need more than just sex with your consort. To achieve the level of sexual magic needed to crush the parasite in your mind, you will need to bring in at least one other sexual partner and indulge in an orgy of multiple orgasms by your partners and yourself. This abundance of sexual energy should boost your magical reservoir enough to break free."

Say what? This fucking bitch wanted me to share my body with another person? Like fucking Hell!

# CHAPTER SEVEN

It was a good thing Auric held me tightly because my fists longed to hit something. "I am so not having an orgy," I yelled. "I have a consort who loves me, thank you very much, and I am so not bringing another girl into the mix. Over my dead fucking body." I'll be damned. I didn't giggle when I said consort. Rage was good for so many things.

The little wizard, unfazed at all by my outburst, shook its head. "Actually, another man would be better, as they put out a greater sexual energy than women do."

My jaw dropped, and I went still for a moment before struggling in Auric's arms, an urge to rip the head off my dad's mage overcoming all reason. I couldn't get free, so I settled for yelling. "You sick little freak. How do you know I can't get enough magic with just one man?"

"Because my magic is sex based, too," said the wrinkled prune, who looked as if she hadn't even thought of sex in a few centuries. "I have a harem of lovers who fulfill me simultaneously to keep my magical reservoirs filled."

That almost did it. Definitely not a pretty mental picture. I almost puked at the thought of it.

Raisin Face kept talking over my grimaces. "Lucky for you, because of who you are, you actually need less sex to fill you up. Of course, you'd need even less if you learned to restrict its flow. I can see it leaking from you even as we speak. This constant leakage is why you need so much sex with your partner."

"How do you know how often we have sex?" I asked suspiciously.

The creature laughed. "I can see it and smell it. And while your lover and you seem to make some potent magic together, you still need more if you want to blast the spell making you fearful. Another man should do the trick. Personally, I find that if the males climax in me at the same time as I achieve orgasm, I harness the greatest amount of power."

She said it so matter-of-factly that it took me a moment to process, and then another not to gag. "I am not indulging in some perverted sex games, not to mention betray my one true love. You—you—sick nympho. You don't know me very well if you think I'd break his heart fucking some other guy. I'd rather put up with nightmares."

The wrinkled face looked at me and

tsked. But I wasn't backing down.

As I glared at her, suddenly her body seemed to get taller. It wore a hood, and it was coming for me, its hand reaching—

I awoke cradled in Auric's arms, his voice rumbling through his chest against my ear. "What is wrong with you?" he snapped. "There was no need to scare her like that."

"Lucifer's daughter must face the truth," said the bitch's voice.

"There's got to be another way," I whispered.

My father frowned at me. "Muriel, you need to calm yourself and listen to the experts here. I am sure Auric will understand. It's just a threesome. No big deal. Your sisters do it all the time."

I looked up at Auric, expecting him to side with me. After all, he loved me. We were soul mates.

"If we have to do it to set you free, then we do it." Said with a stony face and hard voice.

Tears fill my eyes. "Don't—don't you love me?" I hiccuped the words, ashamed at my emotional weakness.

Immediately, he forced my gaze to meet his. But his expression didn't relent. "Of course, I love you. More than anything. But I also can't stand by and watch as the woman I fell in love with is destroyed by a stupid spell, one we have the power to remove. It's just sex, Muriel."

Just? Just!

It was more than that. It was something special, something that brought us closer together. Something for us alone.

I pushed out of his arms and ran, the tears running down my face. How could Auric claim he loved me? He wanted to share me with another man.

Wearing heels didn't mean I couldn't run. I just couldn't run fast enough to escape.

I made it to my father's rock garden before Auric's arms came around me and lifted me up, crushing me against his solid chest.

"Let me go." I kicked my feet uselessly against his strength.

"Never."

"Liar!" I screamed the word at him.

"Listen to me, Muriel. I love you. You and only you. I will always love you."

"Love me so much you want to share me." Bitterly said.

"No, I don't want to fucking share you. It kills me to know this is the only way."

"How do we know it's the only way?" I clung to his shirt and peered at him with tear-streaked cheeks. "Maybe she's lying. We can step up our sex. You know, bring in some toys. A flogger. Anything but someone else. I don't want to ruin what we have." I didn't want to lose him because I knew all too well about jealousy. I'd grown up with avarice all around me. It ate at a person, destroyed them. It also broke up far too many couples.

"The only way we can destroy what we have is by not dealing with this. I love you, baby, but this frightened victim isn't the woman I know. Isn't who you are. If you don't deal with it, it won't be a threesome that ruins us, but your terror. It's not going to get better."

"We don't know that."

"We do!" He practically shouted it. "Stop fucking lying. And admit it. The panic attacks have gotten worse. The nightmares aren't going away. I want you to get better. If it takes sharing you with another man, then I will. If it takes two, three, or four, I still would because, when all is said and done, you are mine."

"But…"

"You. Are. *Mine.*"

He punctuated his claim with action by dragging me against him so his lips swallowed my words, a tender caress that brought more tears to my eyes.

"We'll survive this."

"Will we?" Or would his jealousy tear us

apart?

"We will." Firmly pronounced. "We will do what has to be done, and we will be stronger for it. You will be stronger. It's sex, baby." His lips quirked. "And, for this to work, it has to be mind-blowing sex. Such a hardship."

I scowled at him. "You seem to forget I've only ever been with you, so to me, it is a big deal. Not all of us used to be manwhores."

He snorted. "Just because I've been with women isn't a reason to bring out the claws."

Uh, yes, it was. I wanted to kill every single gal who'd ever tasted his lips. "I have jealously issues. I'm surprised you don't."

"I do. The thought of another guy touching you makes me want to…" He growled, a low and vibrating sound that sent a thrill of pleasure through me. "But jealousy won't cure you."

It was good to know that Auric wasn't as blasé as I'd first thought. However, knowing it did bother him made me ask, "So if we go through with this, how do we choose a victim?"

"Victim?" His brows arched.

"Well, aren't you going to kill him after for having been with me?"

It was what I'd do. Don't judge. I'd totally get spoiled at Christmas by Daddy for showing such irrational and deadly judgment.

"If it were a stranger, then yeah." He scrubbed a hand over his face. "Yeah, I'd probably do something rash. But it doesn't have to be a stranger. Actually I would prefer it not be a stranger."

Immediately my mind flashed to David. As if reading my mind, Auric said his name. "If we do this, I'd like it to be with David."

Guilt, an emotion I wasn't accustomed to, swamped me. The fact that I wanted to immediately agree to his choice seemed wrong, and it worried me for other reasons. "It can't be David."

"Why?"

"Because he's your best friend for one."

"All the more reason to make it him. I trust him."

"Yeah, and what if afterwards you hate him?"

It pleased me when Auric didn't dismiss my concern out of hand. He took a moment to reply. It just wasn't the reply I expected. "I didn't hate him the last time we shared."

Choke. "What?"

A naughty smile pulled at Auric's lips. "You heard me. I've been in a threesome before."

"But you're an angel."

"Was."

"Still. You were trying to get your wings back when I met you. No way you would have gotten involved in a threesome."

"Why not? I'm not a prude."

"Because it's a sin." Ironic coming from her.

Auric snorted. "Sex outside a marriage is a rule the priests concocted, along with God, to stop the coveting that happens among men. It never applied to angels."

"But why would you share? I mean you're both good looking."

"We had just completed a mission, and she was part of the gang. We got all drunk, and one thing led to another." Auric shrugged. "It wasn't that big of a deal."

"Well, it is a big deal to me."

"Considering who your dad is, I find your prudish side kind of endearing." Said with a smirk.

"I am not a prude. I just have…" I almost said morals, and yet, that wasn't entirely true. I just had this ingrained notion of one man, one woman. I'd always believed in a monogamous love and relationship. To me sex was an intimate act. It shocked me to find out that Auric was a little more blasé about sex than I would have expected.

"Is there another reason you don't want it to be David? Do you find him unattractive?"

Were we seriously having this conversation? "No, he's hot. I mean, doable. I mean—Ugh." I glared at him as my foot kept shoving itself deeper into my mouth.

"So you don't have any real objection other than the fact that it won't just be me."

"Isn't that enough?" I grumbled. "And what about David?"

"David will be willing."

Auric sounded so certain, yet I still wasn't convinced.

"I can't decide something like this right now. I need time to think. I mean maybe there's another solution. Some magical artifact or maybe if we marathoned while you were hopped up on Viagra?"

"You do know you're cute when you're in denial, right?"

Um, hello, I was cute all the time.

Auric dipped his head to brush a soft kiss on my lips and whispered, "Think about it, baby, and when you're ready, know I will support and love you through this."

"What if you're wrong?"

"Never." Arrogance from my angel. How easily some sins came to him. Just like he was good at temptation. "Just think," he murmured. "Twice the hands, twice the tongues, and twice the cock, pleasuring you."

His dirty words jump-started my libido,

and arousal flushed my senses. I needed release, and I wanted it now. Being in a public area didn't faze me; actually, the idea of a possible audience excited me.

"I want you," I whispered to him as I tugged at the button on his pants.

The words had no sooner left my mouth than I found myself pressed against a tall rock reminiscent of the ones in Stonehenge. My skirt rode up around my waist as I wrapped my legs around his waist. His impatient fingers ripped away my panties, and he didn't waste time. He thrust into me.

Yes! The walls of my pussy stretched and clung at his invading cock while I dug my fingers into the muscles of his shoulder and urged him on.

"Harder, Auric. Fuck me harder." The rock at my back dug into me, but I welcomed the pain.

His callused fingers clenched the soft flesh of my ass cheeks as he pistoned me with his cock. He buried his face in the curve of my neck, his lips sucking at my tender flesh hard enough to leave a mark. His mark.

Even in the midst of the wild pleasure building in my body, I sensed we were no longer alone. I opened my eyes and looked over Auric's shoulder and saw David at the entrance to the rock garden, his gaze transfixed. Even from here, I could see the bulge in his pants.

Watching us excited him. Our gazes crossed, and instead of embarrassment, or even fleeing to give us privacy, David, instead, did something unexpected. His hand reached down and rubbed across the stretched fabric of his jeans.

There was something titillating about knowing he stroked himself while watching us fucking that made me come. My eyes closed as my orgasm took me, and I shuddered in Auric's arms. I could feel my pussy fisting Auric's cock tightly. So tightly he couldn't resist.

He shouted my name, and his body went rigid, the hot jet of his cum shooting deep inside. Marking me. Claiming me.

When I found the strength to open my eyes, I noticed David had left and, being a bad girl, wondered if he'd left to finish what he'd started.

A part of me wondered that I wasn't bothered by the fact that he'd watched us and that he was using us as his fantasy to get off. So dirty. So fun. I couldn't say it was wrong, though, because I'd gotten such a thrill from it. And I admit it. I was intrigued by the thought of it happening again.

*Except maybe next time he could join in.*

Shudder. I blamed Auric for planting the thought. But I wouldn't give in. Not without a fight. A naked one.

# CHAPTER EIGHT

Not much was said while Auric and I straightened our clothes. Knowing how my father eschewed manners, and not wanting to see or speak to anyone until I could sort things out, we left, gathering David on our way.

If the naughty kitty had tugged one off, he showed no sign of it. Caught in my tumultuous thoughts, I said not a word as we passed through the portal Auric sketched back to our apartment. Or at least the hall outside of it. While Auric could draw one within it, the magic shielding of our place didn't allow for one back in.

Exhausted, mentally and physically, I crawled into bed while David and Auric whispered on the other side of the apartment. I thought about listening in, but honestly, I could guess what Auric was telling him, and I just couldn't face it.

How does someone have that conversation? "Hey there, best friend, mind joining me and the girlfriend in a threesome? We'll take turns fucking and making her come." Just the thought of it boggled the mind. And what pissed me off even more—

thinking about it made me hot. Made me wonder if perhaps Auric was right. If it could cure me, then why was I hesitating about inviting David into our bed?

Attraction wasn't a problem. David was an extremely good-looking guy. Curiosity also raised its nose. I'd only ever been with Auric sexually. What would another man taste like? Feel like? Could anyone else even come close to giving me the same kind of pleasure?

Just wondering made me sick with guilt. Was this truly me thinking these thoughts, or was it my magic tainting my thought process?

As I lay awake, mind churning, I heard the door shut with a soft click. A moment later, the blankets were pulled back and a very naked Auric climbed into bed.

"Are you awake?" he murmured.

I debated answering. Should I feign sleep? I really didn't want to rehash the crap we'd learned in Hell.

Thankfully, Auric wasn't interested in starting another painful discussion. Instead, he gathered me in his arms and sought my mouth hungrily. I clung to him, desperation in my kisses as I sought to show him how much I loved him. How much he meant to me.

He grabbed my hands and pinned them above my head, making my back arch and thrusting out my breasts. His lips left mine to kiss my neck and bite it. Gently he sucked me, marking me again, something that pleased me to no end. I'd wear my pair of hickeys with pride tomorrow.

Scraping the bristly edge of his jaw down the delicate skin of my neck, he made his way down to my tits. My nipples puckered at the feel of his warm breath tickling them. He rubbed his face across the soft skin of my breasts, and he even scraped my nipple, making me gasp. Auric had the art of teasing down to a science, and I loved it. I quivered under his sensuous onslaught, my sex wet and aching, my breathing rapid and shallow.

Finally he took my breast in his mouth, his hot, moist mouth working my flesh, devouring it and leaving it damp and quivering. He pulled away and did the same thing to my other breast, my moist skin pimpling in the cooler air, making me shiver all over. He licked a path between my breasts, a wet trail of saliva that made no sense until he climbed up my body, still holding my hands, and straddling my chest, he slid his cock between my breasts using the slick path he'd created. Oh, how naughty.

I tilted my chin down and licked the tip of his swollen head when it came close, and Auric closed his eyes for a moment and shuddered. He slid back and then forward again, and I opened my mouth wide and, this time, clamped my lips around the entirety of his engorged shaft. Back and forth he slid his cock, each time sliding it a little farther into my mouth.

This excited me. I felt at his mercy. His hands held mine tightly, and his weight straddling me held me down. I could suck his cock, but only when he brought it near enough.

Holding my two hands pinned above my head in just one of his, he reached back with his other and fingered me, his callused finger parting my wet folds and finding my sensitive clit. I wanted to cry out with the pleasure of it, but he gagged me with his cock. I sucked him eagerly as his finger stroked me, raising my body to a fever pitch of excitement. When I thought I would bite down to get his attention, unable to bear the torture anymore, he pulled his throbbing cock from my mouth and slid down my body until the head of his engorged shaft rubbed against my wet lips. I thrust my hips up just as he plunged his cock in, and we met with a hard clash that had me grabbing him and clawing his back. He pulled himself out, teasing me again with the swollen tip, then dove back in, establishing a rhythm that kept increasing in tempo. Mindless, I felt my pussy give one last tight squeeze then explode. I could vaguely feel him pumping into me, but floating on an orgasmic cloud, my whole body quivering, I found it took too much energy to open my eyes and watch him.

But he would not be ignored. I felt him move, and he straddled my upper chest again. He fed the tip of his cock between my lips, slick with my own juices, and I opened wider, taking his hard length. With a shudder, he came in my mouth, and I swallowed because, after all, we all knew the difference between like and love was measured in whether a girl spat or swallowed.

He moved to the side and collapsed on the bed. Strong, sure hands grabbed me and pulled me over so I lay sprawled on top of him. Snuggling, I wondered how he could even think of betraying what we had. When we came together, it was magical. Special. Or was I just deluded? Was sex like this for everyone? If I fucked David, would I achieve the same heights? I fell asleep troubled.

And later woke screaming, the pain so vivid that I cried and thrashed on the bed. Auric held me down until I calmed.

He kissed my sweaty forehead. "I can't stand to see you suffering like this, baby."

"I'm fine now. Already gone." Only a partial lie. The dream pain lingered, but it was fading.

Auric frowned. "You can't keep going on like this. This is nuts. Let me call David."

"Yes, because I'm so in the mood for a great big ol' orgy right now." I felt about as sexy as a dirty gym sock and probably smelled as pretty, too, with the acrid stench of my fear still flavoring my skin.

"So we plan for it tomorrow."

"Or never."

"Why must you be so fucking stubborn?"

"Because I want you to spank me?" I batted my lashes at him, but he didn't melt.

"I don't see why you're so against even trying what those mages suggested. I mean, come on, we both know you're going to love it."

Yeah, I probably would, but that wasn't the point.

I hit him in the solar plexus, and while he wheezed, I rolled out of bed and stalked into the bathroom, shouting over my shoulder at him. "I am not having a fucking threesome. So stop throwing your buddy at me!"

Then I was struck by a thought, and I poked my head back out of the bathroom and looked at him speculatively. "Are you bi?"

The look on his face was almost comedic. "Most assuredly not," he sputtered.

"Just making sure. You seem awfully keen on getting another guy to join us."

Auric came off the bed, six foot something of yumminess, taut with anger. "I am not into men, nor am I that keen, as you say, to share you. You're mine. *Mine.*" He growled the word. "But part of protecting you means doing shit I never imagined, like taking you to bed and seeing another guy's hands on you. Another dick fucking you. It kills me. Fucking kills me to have to share you. But I will do it because I refuse to watch you waking up screaming for the rest of your life. I won't have it."

"They're just nightmares."

"It's more than fucking nightmares," he shouted, "and you know it. Have you even considered how vulnerable this spell makes you? You faint at the mention of his name. You tremble at the thought. Don't you realize if this so-called master shows up, you'll be useless?" I quivered, and my knees gave out. Auric caught me before I hit the floor. "And there you go, proving my point. Baby, you've got to see it's the only way. If I can handle it, why can't you?"

"Because I'm afraid you'll look at me differently after." I voiced the truth and could just imagine my father wincing in Hell.

"Never. Muriel, this isn't about you going behind my back and cheating. This is you accepting what needs to be done. Done for both of our sakes."

"I don't like it."

"That's fine. But you need to stop fighting it. I know I asked before if it was David you objected to and you said no, but maybe you'd find it easier with someone else. Would you perhaps prefer Christopher?"

"Ugh. No." Bed a guy with the same name as my estranged half-brother? Even I wasn't that depraved. "If I had to choose, I'd choose David. But I don't want to choose. I just want you."

"And I'm not enough."

I caught the flash of pain on his face, the utter sadness and sense of futility that he didn't hide. He walked away from me, and I couldn't help but slump as I pondered something new.

It hadn't occurred to me to look at my whole 'fraidy cat situation from his point of view; after all, the world revolved around me. However, Auric and I were a couple. He was the one soothing me every night. The one worrying every time I left the house. The one who'd started out dating a kick-ass chick, only to end up with a big fat pussy—the cowardly kind, not the sexy, pink, delicious one.

I stared at him stiffly going through the motions of making us coffee and breakfast. In that moment, I realized that this had to be hard for him, too, but dammit, I didn't want to fuck anyone else. I had old-fashioned notions on fidelity, and they involved one man and one woman. Not to mention I was terrified if I went down the path of erotic pleasure. What if I didn't want to come back? What if I tasted the bliss that came from having two lovers and could never content myself with one again?

Did I dare risk it all?

Auric said not a word to me during breakfast, but I could see speculation in his eyes, and it bugged me. He left to run some errands, and I did laundry. Boring, but even Satan's daughter liked to have clean underwear.

When Auric returned, he had a decisive air about him.

"I'm going on a trip to gather some intel," he announced while packing a bag.

I dropped the socks I was sorting. "When do we leave?" I was eager for some action and glad he'd forgotten the topic of threesomes for now.

"You're not going. It's too dangerous in your current mental state."

I glared at him. I hated it when he pulled the chauvinistic shit with me. "Then you shouldn't be going either."

Being the recipient of a very masculine

and haughty look that seemed to say, *How dare you tell me what to do?* brought out the imp in me—and my tongue.

"Are you going to even try and be mature about this?"

"No. I don't see why it's okay for you to put yourself in danger but I can't."

"Muriel, this is not open for discussion. I want you safe. So I'm going alone."

"I don't like it." I planted my hands on my hips, a pose I'm sure many a nagging girlfriend and wife had adopted over the centuries.

"I didn't ask you to like it. I'm leaving as soon as your guard arrives."

"When will you be back?"

"I don't know."

A vague answer, which struck me as suspicious, especially since he seemed to suddenly have difficulty looking me in the eye. Given our recent fight and his paranoia over my security, I couldn't understand why he had to go.

"Why you? Can't someone else go?" What I didn't say was, what if I need you? I worried about having to use my magic to protect myself. Once used, I'd need to recharge. Without Auric around, I'd have to masturbate, which, while pleasant, didn't even come close to filling my energy stores. Not to mention, we'd not spent a night apart since we'd hooked up a month ago.

"It's got to be me. I don't trust anyone else."

I shivered with the understanding that this mission had something to do with Azazel and… I just wouldn't think about that.

He kissed me fiercely, as if he wanted to brand my soul with the feel of him. Not that I minded. I liked it when he got a little rough.

He pulled back and looked at me with serious eyes. "Promise me you'll be careful."

"As careful as usual," I quipped.

"Muriel, I'm serious. Don't do anything foolish."

"Who me?" I widened my eyes, attempting innocence and laughed at the pained look on his face. "Fine, I promise. No going to Hell or kicking demon ass by myself. Happy?"

"No, which is why I'm having David stay here while I'm gone."

"Is this your way of getting me to come around to the idea of inviting him into a threesome?"

"No, this is my way of keeping you safe and out of trouble."

"A babysitter?" I squeaked. "I don't need David keeping an eye on me. I'm a big girl. I can take care of myself."

"Just humor me, please. It'll make me feel better if David's close by. Promise me you'll use him if you need him." Auric's eyes and tone were bland, making me even more suspicious. He was up to something. Something I probably wouldn't like.

"I'm not making any more promises. David can walk me to and from work so long as he behaves and doesn't get in my way."

"David's also going to be sleeping on the couch. You need someone to wake you from the nightmares. He's also here to protect you, and if you don't listen to him, he's got my permission to spank you."

"David wouldn't," I said assuredly.

"He will if he doesn't want me to geld him when I get back." Auric's eyes glowed with menace.

A shiver went through me, and I was instantly aroused. What could I say? He was hot when he got all bad boy.

"I don't suppose he can cook?" I asked hopefully.

Auric grinned. "Not like I can, baby. Don't worry. He's a master at ordering in, and if you want fresh meat, then he's your man."

I thought of some poor fluffy bunny being brought to me like a cat brings a bird to its owner and grimaced. "Ugh. No thank you. I'll stick to frozen dinners and take out, thank you very much. Do you really have to go?"

"It's only for a few days." Auric wrapped his arms around me one last time. "I've got a lead on something I've been looking into."

"This isn't too dangerous, is it?"

"Nope. Piece of cake."

Not reassuring. I'd met some deadly triple chocolate cakes in my time.

I grabbed him by the hair and dragged his mouth down to mine, my tongue slipping between his lips to dance with his. Large hands reached down to cup my ass cheeks and squeeze them, and I pressed myself into him, feeling his erection pressing against my lower belly.

"Let's go for one more quickie," I panted.

Of course, that was when some fool decided to knock on the door. Auric tore his lips away from mine and, with a chagrined look, said, "I'll be back before you know it. I love you, Muriel. No matter what. Remember that."

"I love you, too."

I could only hug myself, already feeling forlorn, as he grabbed his backpack and headed for the door. I saw him exchange a few words with David, who had arrived to babysit me. Then he left.

Having no shame where he was concerned, I scurried to the window to watch as he and Christopher headed away—away from me.

Something about his departure nagged at me, a sense of something not right, but at least with him gone, he wouldn't be bugging me about a threesome.

Looking at David prowling the loft I shared with Auric, I found myself eyeing him in a new light. It wasn't just Auric's insistence I consider him that was to blame. I also wasn't sure how to stop myself from recalling, make that fantasizing, about a voyeuristic David joining in.

A big fat light bulb went off and blinded me with realization. I suddenly understood Auric's devious plan. With him gone and David underfoot, he hoped I'd change my mind about the whole threesome thing. If I got to know David and fell in lust with him, then maybe I'd agree to let David put his sausage in my bun. Not likely. I'd sew my lips shut first, both pairs if needed.

With that knowledge fueling my thoughts, I decided to establish some ground rules. "Now that Auric is gone, we need to talk about what's going to happen, starting with you not sleeping here."

"Yes, I am." Chin set stubbornly—AKA super cute—David crossed muscular arms over his chest.

"Oh no you're not. Listen, Auric has gone overboard with this whole protection bit." I wouldn't let on that I'd figured out the master plan. "I'm safe here. The place is spelled against demons." I threw the kitty a bone. "So let's forget the whole sleepover part of the plan and stick to you showing up to walk me to and from work."

With an implacable stare, David said, "I'm staying here until Auric gets back."

I stomped my foot, piqued at not getting my way. This whole not-being-obeyed thing was getting annoying. I could see why my dad went on rampages. "Dammit. I am not a child. I wish you and Auric would stop treating me like one."

"Keeping you safe isn't treating you like a child. I'd say it shows foresight and care on his part."

"It's annoying."

"Suck it up, princess."

Had David really said that to me? Judging by the smirk on his lips and twinkle in his eyes, yes. Jerk.

Only one thing to do. I stuck my tongue out at him. Treat me like a child and I'd act like one. He might have won the first round, but I wasn't done yet. I'd nag at him again later. Eventually I'd get my way. Just ask my dad. I rocked at getting what I wanted.

For the rest of that afternoon, I ignored David as best as I could, not easy when you've got a six-foot-something male prowling your apartment. At least sensing my mood, he stayed quiet.

As the afternoon waned, I got ready for work and wore something that matched my mood—a black tube skirt that hit mid-thigh with a mini slit on one side, a bright red silk blouse with matching lipstick, and my hair coiled on top of my head. Oh, and to finish the ensemble, black panty hose that had the seam up the back with garters and strappy black sandals. It was an outfit determined to cause trouble.

Our walk to work was quiet and uneventful. David probably sensed me still simmering and wisely didn't tempt my temper. I still couldn't believe what Auric had planned. More and more I suspected his leave taking and leaving me alone with David was his way of convincing me to drop my panties and invite him on in.

I bet he hadn't counted on my stubbornness. I'd spite myself to win, something Auric and David would both soon learn.

But it was hard to stay mad at David, even if he did hang around the bar area all evening. How could I be pissed when he did his best to help? Giving Perry a hand serving drinks. Taking care of the drunks and being generally useful. Even more astonishing, he ignored the come-hither glances of the dryads who waitressed. Not too many men could resist their willowy shapes and sensual invitation.

And yes I noticed. Noticed far too much about David.

To my annoyance, I found myself glancing over at him more than once. It wasn't as if he had Auric's magnetic aura, but he did have some appeal—the forbidden fruit variety. Or at least forbidden by my standards.

When I closed up for the night, David silently handed me my jacket. I had an urge to get in his face and scream just to see if he'd react. I mean, seriously, my fuming had to be driving him nuts. Auric would have thrown me over his shoulder by now and paddled my bottom had I tried this stunt with him. Oh, how I missed him already.

A loud sigh escaped me, and I saw David slide a look sideways at me, but he kept walking, hands shoved deep into his pockets.

I stopped walking. David went a few paces before he realized I wasn't beside him and whirled around.

"Doesn't it bother you at all?" I asked him point-blank.

"What?"

"I know what you guys are up to, and it's not going to work."

"Really? Care to enlighten me as to what we're up to?" He looked at me with an innocent expression I didn't believe for one minute.

I stomped my foot. "Stop playing dumb."

"Look—" David started to speak, only to stop as a shadow wrapped itself around his neck and choked him.

Shit! Demons. I'd been so busy being annoyed I hadn't heard or smelled them approaching. Cursing my stupidity, I pulled a long knife from the sheath that ran down my spine and whirled, ready to kick some demon ass.

Two squat forms approached, the sheen of their red skin worrying me. Only one type of demon bore that color. Fire demons. Fuck. It meant calling flames to my blade wouldn't help. But the sharp edge would still slice flesh.

Never one to give up, I dropped into a partially crouched fighting stance. My short skirt rode high on my thighs, showing off my black lace garters and the tops of my legs. I saw the demons glance down—males were so easy to distract—and I struck first. Swirling my blade, I ducked in and scored a line across the chest of one of them.

Dancing back, I felt like shouting, "Ha," but my glee was short-lived. The demon ignored the scratch and, along with his friend, came at me from both sides. Unable to watch them both, I spun a foot out behind me, my stiletto heel sinking into something soft and fleshy. Eew. However, now wasn't the time to worry about demon blood on my shoes as I parried the swinging fist of the other demon with my long blade.

I could hear snarling and spitting behind me and knew David had let his kitty out to play, but these demons were tough. Built as soldiers for Hell, they were much more resilient than other varieties of demon.

I found myself tiring, my movements getting slower as I parried and thrust in an unending rhythm. A slash across my mid-section, slicing open my favorite red silk blouse, brought on the magical trance.

As on other occasions when I found myself in mortal peril, words of power appeared in my mind, and I spoke, their terrible energy lashing out, drawing upon the magic stored within me until, like a dried husk that had no more juice to give, I collapsed.

# CHAPTER NINE

The pavement reached up to slap me as my legs refused to hold my weight. Limper than an overcooked noodle, I couldn't even brace as the hard ground rushed to say hello.

Arms wrapped around me from behind and caught me inches before my face would have become intimately acquainted with the sidewalk.

"Are you okay, Muriel?" David asked.

Not really, but I refused to admit it. "Just dandy."

"So I can let you go?"

"No!"

He laughed. "Not so fine after all."

"I will be. Just give me a minute. I am going to assume, given we're able to chitchat without interruption, that the demons are all gone."

"Yes. Whatever you did, it turned them all into dust. But you look like shit."

Gee, talk about an ego booster. "I'll be fine. I just need..." Sex. But with Auric gone, that wouldn't happen.

Shit. Talk about an inconvenient time for him to take off. But I'd manage. I'd just have to masturbate. I refused to listen to my nagging inner voice that reminded self-pleasure would give me only a fraction of my power back, not to mention I'd have to do it in the bathroom, given my temporary roommate.

*You could always fuck David*, my insidious mind whispered.

No. I was pretty sure when Auric left he'd meant for me to get used to David and the idea, not actually *do* David. But I had to admit this whole needing-sex situation to power my magical batteries really sucked. Auric hadn't even been gone a day, and already, I had used up all my power.

Great, now I'd be practically useless until he came back. I'd survive; I had before. Of course, before I met Auric, I'd only had a few assassination attempts, not concentrated efforts to take me out. But on the bright side, at least I couldn't complain my life was boring.

David shifted behind me, his arms changing their grip on my limp spaghetti body, pulling me upright and back against him. Suddenly, I became aware of the fact that David wore not a stitch of clothing—and he seemed to be very happy to see me.

My cheeks burned hotly, and I pushed away from him. "I can stand on my own," I declared. My good old friend Murphy, who was always waiting for moments like these, swooped in with a vengeance, and I fell over in an ungraceful heap.

Without a word—why bother when I could so clearly hear Auric laugh and call me idiot in my mind?—David picked me up again, this time cradling me princess style in his arms. This brought my face in close proximity to the smooth skin of his chest and scent, a musky masculine, yummy smell that someone could have bottled for an outrageous price.

"Put me down," I demanded, even as my body melted in his arms.

"No." He spoke in a firmer tone than I'd ever heard from him before.

Why had he chosen now of all times to get a backbone? "This isn't appropriate." A prim response and ironic, too, given my parentage, but somehow, as innocuous as this was, I felt as though I was betraying Auric.

I loved Auric. I never wanted to do anything that would make him doubt that, whether he wanted me to want David or not. Damn, this whole thing was bloody confusing. My poor little brain hurt.

Not listening to my protests, David carried me to the loft. I didn't know what was the biggest miracle; us not running into anybody while a naked six footish man carted me around or the ground not opening up to swallow me from embarrassment.

I tried to get him to put me down a few times, but David, in an uncharacteristically stubborn stance—one I'd have to disabuse him of once I got my strength back—refused to, leaving me fuming in his arms. If he thought his gallant act would make me drop my panties for him, he had another thing coming, even if said panties were actually wet.

Think anyone would believe I peed myself? Or would the honey scent of my arousal give it away?

We finally reached the inside of the loft, where David deposited me onto the couch.

"Can you leave now?" I asked. I was tired, drained, and really fucking aroused. I needed him to leave before I did something stupid. Before I did something I'd regret.

I could sense the empty hole in myself where my magic usually resided, and damn was it hungry. It didn't care if David wasn't my main squeeze. It wanted stimulation, and it wanted it now.

But this new stubborn David looked at me with raised brows. "Are you nuts? I am not going anywhere. We just got attacked by demons, and you're about as strong as a newborn kitten right now. No way am I leaving you alone."

"Pussy." I hissed at him. Why not? I felt

petty.

"Listen." David paced back and forth, his nude body slimmer than Auric's but just as well toned. I kept glancing away—from temptation. Chocolate had nothing on his smooth skin, but he purposely walked into my line of sight, distracting me. His nudity called to the depleted magical side of me, an almost living entity that screamed, *Fuck him. We're weak.*

Realizing I was eyeing David like a lion eyes a gazelle—hungrily—I forced my stare onto my toes—they could use a pedi—and dug my nails into my palms. Through the pounding blood that roared, I tried to pay attention to David as he talked.

"Auric had a talk with me before he left."

"About?" Stupid question since I knew. I also knew I didn't want to hear this and wondered if I stuck my fingers in my ears and hummed whether David would get the point and go away.

"He was afraid that you'd be forced to use your powers while he was gone. He told me how you need to replenish your magic, through sex. He didn't just leave me behind to guard you, Muriel. He left me behind to act as a surrogate for him in case you needed to fill your magic back up."

"Liar. I know what his plan is. He wants

me to get used to the idea of having a threesome to get rid of the spell in my head. There's no way he'd want me to betray him by sleeping with his best friend while he was gone. You're lying."

"You know I'm not. It's precisely because I'm his best friend that he asked me. I know you love him, and he loves you. But your power needs sex. Not love. He asked me to give it to you while he was gone if you needed it."

I wanted to scream he lied. I wanted to tell him to get out. But I knew he told the truth. Auric had pretty much said it in not so many words when he'd left me, on purpose I now realized.

I laughed, the edge of it somewhat hysterical. "How kind of him. And you, such a good friend, agreeing to fuck me as if my feelings don't count."

"It's not like that, Muriel."

"Isn't it?" I shook my head. "No. I won't do it. Put some clothes on."

"Why?" David stopping to stand in front of me, his cock half erect in a nest of blond curls.

"Because." Sometimes that was the only answer.

"I think you want me to get dressed and leave because you know I'm right. I'm a shifter, Muriel. I know you want me. I can smell it."

"That's gross."

"That's the truth."

"I hate the truth."

"Hate it all you want. You still want this."

The jerk let his dick bob in front of me.

I licked my lips and fought a temptation to lean forward and touch it. My magic, like an alter ego, struggled within me as I fought the arousal flushing my body. I bit my lip hard, tasting blood, and turned my face.

To my shame, I felt hot tears run down my cheeks. I hated what my magic was doing to me. I loved Auric. I wanted to wait for him. I had to be stronger than the magic. I couldn't give in. "I can't. I just can't. If you don't mind, I'm going to bed."

With heavy limbs, I dragged myself to the bathroom to change into some nightclothes—because tonight, of all nights, sleeping naked just wasn't a good idea.

My energy-sapped body screamed at me to get some sex, some stimulation, anything, but I found myself too mentally and physically exhausted to listen. A T-shirt and shorts felt confining compared to my usual sleep wear—nothing at all. I clambered into the gigantic bed, alone.

Scalding tears leaked from my eyes and

soaked my pillow. Auric might be convinced we had to betray what we had, but I'd show him it didn't have to be that way. I'd force myself to be strong. I would resist, and when Auric returned, we'd look for another way to cure me. A way that didn't involve another man.

And didn't make my head and heart hurt so much.

# CHAPTER TEN

The dream started as it usually did, with me alone in Hell. Where it changed was how long the agony went on.

I was pain's bitch, and it practically cackled as I writhed and screamed, wishing I could die. Then I felt comforting arms wrap around me, holding me tight, pulling me from the clutching grip of the nightmare.

Auric had returned. He'd saved me from the horror nestled in my mind.

As I panted, I snuggled into the safety and warmth of his arms and body, the memory of the agony slowly receding. When I stopped whimpering and shaking, I took a deep breath and smelled... David, not Auric.

Horrified, I tried to push out of his arms, but he tightened his grip.

"Shhh. Calm down, Muriel."

Calm down? A man was in my bed, and he wasn't my boyfriend. "Why are you holding me?" I asked, unable to hide my indignation.

"You wouldn't stop screaming, and I couldn't wake you up."

Good reason. But still, it wasn't proper. "I'm fine now. You can let me go." Never mind that it felt almost as nice as when Auric held me. It was wrong.

David, however, didn't listen. I swear my bad influence was starting to rub off. What happened to nice boys who listened when girls told them to fuck off?

"How do you stand it?" he asked.

"Because there's no other choice."

"Not true. There is a solution. Don't forget, I was there. I heard that witch lady tell you what to do."

"She wants me to have sex with Auric and another guy."

"I know. Seems easy enough, so excuse me if I don't understand why you allow yourself to suffer this every night if you don't have to."

"I do have to because it isn't easy. You're talking about betraying the man I love. Given the choice between nightmares and possibly losing Auric, there's no choice. I won't risk it."

"But there is no risk. Don't you get it? Auric isn't going anywhere, and if he does, it will be because you're too stubborn to do what has to be done. Are you really that selfish and blind that you can't see how this spell that's torturing you is killing him? I hadn't quite understood how bad it was until tonight. Do you know how helpless I felt when I couldn't wake you and were screaming like that? Can you imagine how Auric feels? And you've been doing this to him for, what, a month now? How cruel are you?"

I wanted to say "I'm not cruel, he is," but the look of horror on David's face stopped me.

How would I feel if it was Auric in unbearable agony? Would I not do anything to stop it? I'd offered my life for his not so long ago to stop him from being hurt. Now all he asked of me was to do something that my body would enjoy, something he approved of and would participate in to save me.

I really disliked middle-of-the-night epiphanies. They made me nasty.

"Just go away, David. I'm not fucking you, so forget it." I turned on my side and closed my eyes, pretending sleep. David sighed loudly, but he didn't budge.

"You know, Muriel," he said after a while, "I'm not doing this for the sex. I'm doing this because my best friend is hurting, and unlike you, I'd like to see it stop. Let me ask you something?"

"What now?" I growled.

"If you're dirty, you shower, right? If you're hungry, you eat. If you're tired, you sleep. Why is it, when your magic asks for a refill, you treat it differently than the rest of your bodily needs?"

"You don't know what you're talking about."

"Really?" Apparently David was in the mood to talk and not leave because he made himself more comfortable beside me on top of the covers.

A part of me wanted to peek and see if he was still naked, but I controlled myself— barely.

"When the full moon hits, did you know I have to shift and hunt something? And when I say hunt, I mean, I need to find something living and tear into it with fangs until its blood runs down my throat."

"Oh, that is so gross!" I exclaimed.

"Yes, it is. And it took me years to come to grips with the fact that it is part of who I am. I used to fight it, calling myself all kinds of names, castigating myself. Then Auric came into my life and asked why I fought the nature of my beast. I told him it was gross. Inhumane. He reminded me I was a shapeshifter, with needs. He also pointed out that the creatures I hunted weren't weak and that I didn't torture them needlessly. I went after other aggressive carnivores, and when I killed, I did so quickly and with mercy."

"I'm still not seeing the connection." Hoping he'd continue to talk, fascinated in spite of myself.

"You keep equating sex with love and commitment instead of looking at it as a basic need that needs to be met. When you have sex with Auric, sure, get all emotional about it. When you have sex for magic, leave the feelings out of it and do what needs to be done."

"I don't like how my magic needs to be refueled."

"Nobody said you had to." I felt the whisper of a touch running up my back, a ghostly sensation that made me shiver. "But there will be times Auric isn't around. Times you'll need to recharge. Do you think he'd thank you for your morals if it leads to you dying because you had no magic to save yourself?"

No, he'd probably hunt down my ghost and punish it for being so fucking stupid.

"So you're saying I should think of sex like food."

"I think you need to come to grips with who you are, and do what has to be done."

"With you."

"With me."

Funny how he didn't hesitate or give me an option to use someone else. I might have qualms about using him for sex, but he obviously didn't.

"If I did agree, there would be no

kissing." I couldn't believe I was even contemplating this, but I couldn't deny that the sleep I'd gotten hadn't given me back my strength. On the contrary, I felt weaker than ever.

"Ahh, *Pretty Woman* still lives when it comes to sex without strings. That's fine," he said, agreeing easily. He swept my hair aside, and his warm lips touched the back of my neck.

I shuddered, and desire flared to life in between my legs.

"I haven't agreed yet." Words that belied the fact that my body thrummed with anticipation.

David nipped my ear and whispered, "What else would you have me promise?"

"I don't love you, and I don't want you to love me."

"No emotions, just sex between friends to help you out. Is that all?"

"Are you sure this is what Auric wanted?"

"I wouldn't lie about something like this." I could hear the truth in his words.

I didn't speak, just nodded, his light caresses already starting to feed the hole that my magic resided in. I tried to roll over, but he kept me pinned to the bed on my stomach and kept nibbling the tender flesh of my neck.

He pulled up the fabric of my T-shirt,

and lifting my arms, he removed it. He left my shorts on and began exploring the skin of my back, his mouth alternating between caressing and nipping. I could sense him over me, straddling my buttocks, but not sitting on me. His hands ran down my sides lightly, and I restrained a giggle.

It tickled.

He ran them back up again and slid them under my body just beneath my breasts. His hands, smoother than Auric's, cupped my breasts, and even smooshed flat, he managed to tweak my nipples and roll them between his fingers. Something that made me gnaw my lip and shiver.

I gasped when he lay himself full length on me. His naked skin was feverishly hot against mine, the hardness of his erection poking at my backside, the flimsy material of my shorts the only thin barrier stopping it from touching me.

My heart wavered for a moment when I felt his hands on the waistband of my shorts, pulling them down, but my magic screamed, Yes! My magic and desire won. I couldn't stop him now. The coiling heat inside me needed relief.

My bottoms discarded, he lay back on top of me, skin to skin, his shaft a burning rod lying within the crevice of my buttocks. He nibbled at my neck again, a sensitive spot of mine, making me arch back against him. His musky scent filled my senses and acted like an airborne pheromone that brought out an animalistic side I didn't know I had.

I mewled and bucked against his hard-on. He responded by nipping my neck and wrapping an arm around my waist. He lifted me into a hands-and-knees position and pushed apart my thighs. Having never been taken like this, but aware of its bestial origin, I panted, waiting and wanting. His fingers probed me first, two long and smooth fingers that slid between my wet lips and made me cry out when they reached deep inside and touched my G-spot. He stroked it with his fingers, making me writhe and moan.

When I would have collapsed on the bed, flat on my stomach again, he slapped my ass and pulled me back up. The sting excited, even as it shocked me. I would have never taken David to be an aggressive lover.

Again his fingers touched me. I whimpered, my body taut with need. Finally he stopped his torture, and with a swift move, he sheathed his cock inside me.

Strange as it seemed for just a moment, I compared the feel of him to Auric. Long, like Auric, but not quite as thick. As if to compensate for his girth, he reached under and found my clit. I bucked against him, and I heard him hiss, not in pain but in pleasure. David was not as cool about this as he'd been leading me to believe. Feeling more confident and so close to my climax, I moved my hips back against him while he rubbed my clit. He pounded me in steady strokes, his body slapping up against my buttocks making me grunt as he drove himself deep. He leaned over me and pushed down on my back, collapsing my upper arms so my face and upper part of my chest lay on the bed while my ass still hovered in the air. This position seemed to allow him to go even deeper, and I moaned as he banged up against my womb, my secret spot of pleasure.

I clawed at the sheets, feeling my body approaching that familiar pleasure plateau, and with a small cry, I crested it, my sex squeezing tight around his cock. With a hoarse cry, David pulled out, and I felt him spurt his seed over my back.

While my body calmed down, I realized two things. One, while I had enjoyed this bout with David and felt my magic somewhat replenished, it had been nothing like the earth-shattering lovemaking I experienced with Auric. And two, cooling jizz on my back was so gross!

"Eew!" I screeched. "What the Hell did

you shoot onto my back for? Get a towel."

Immediately, he hopped off the bed. I watched, still with interest, the naked movement of David's ass as he bolted for the bathroom and came back with something to wipe me up.

"Sorry," he said, his cheeks that adorable shade of red. "You have a thing with kissing. I have a thing with coming inside a girl. I don't want to get you accidentally pregnant."

Pregnancy? Hell no. I took a pill for that.

"Thanks, just, next time, warn me, would you?" Oops. I'd said next time.

And I guess there would be a next time if I wanted to rid myself of the curse in my head.

As a matter of fact, there was no reason now not to do the threesome, that was if Auric really was fine with all this.

*Please let everything be fine.* The world did not want to see what I was capable of if my heart got broken.

# CHAPTER ELEVEN

The next evening, Auric walked into the bar looking dangerous and handsome. Back much sooner than I'd been led to believe.

I flashed a dark glare at David, who at least had the grace to duck his head.

I'd been set up. Forced to have sex with someone. Okay, not forced, and I'd enjoyed it, but still, I'd been manipulated.

Pissed, I felt a dangerous rage rise in me, and I fled my post behind the bar, lest my fiery eyes betray my parentage to my patrons. Most of them knew or guessed, but still, I didn't like to advertise it.

I'd barely closed the door when it opened and Auric entered with a wary step. "Hey, baby. I'm back."

"Don't you fucking baby me, you bastard!" I yelled. I grabbed and threw the nearest thing at hand—my favorite mug—at his head.

Auric ducked, and it smashed against the door. "Aren't you happy to see me?"

Yes, but I wouldn't give him the satisfaction of telling him, especially since my happiness at his return was being choked by my anger. "You set me up."

"You didn't give me a choice. You wouldn't see reason." His puny explanation and shrug didn't hold a shred of apology.

"So, because I wouldn't spread my legs for your friend, you sent demons after me? Did you seriously do it on purpose to make sure I'd use up all my power and have no choice but to fuck David?"

The expression on his face tightened. "No, I didn't send them after you. They were real assassins, or kidnappers. We're still not entirely sure. The other ones we caught never did say why they were after you."

His words froze me. "What others?"

"The ones your father and I have been protecting you from. The ones the bodyguards he assigned to shadow you have been dispatching."

Hold on a second. "There have been other assassins sent after me? How did I not know this?"

"Because the guards your dad assigned have been taking care of them."

And I had been oblivious the entire time. "But they didn't kill the demons last night."

"No, because we chose to pull the guards back to see what would happen."

What happened was…"You forced me to fight them? You wanted me to use my magic?"

I gaped at him. "What happened to protecting me?" I thought he had my back—and my pussy and my heart. Yet, he'd thrown me to the demons.

"You were never in any danger. I was close by, making sure you'd be safe."

I saw red, and I knew my eyes were glowing. "You mean," I growled, taking a step towards him, "that you were nearby the entire time and did nothing?"

"You're always saying you can take care of yourself. I let you prove it."

The smug smile on his face just made things worse, even with his backwards compliment. "You knew I'd have to use my magic. Knew I'd drain myself to the point I'd need recharging. In other words, you manipulated things so that I was forced to turn to David when I was weak. How could you?" How could he betray our love like that?

That level of subterfuge was something I expected from my father, and other residents of Hell, not my lover.

A flash of pain touched his eyes, but just as quickly, it disappeared, and he regarded me stonily. "I could because it had to be done. You left me no choice with your stubborn refusal to accept the inevitable."

"Inevitable? You made me cheat on you."

Again, a hint of a flinch. He wasn't as

unaffected as he claimed. "What happened with David was only sex."

"Only sex," I scoffed. "Doesn't it bother you at all that another man saw me naked? Touched me?"

Auric's face tightened with anger. "Of course it bothers me. I am not immune to jealousy, but let me ask you something. Did your souls touch when you fucked?"

My turn to recoil at his crudeness. "No."

"Do you love me any less?"

Did I? I examined my emotions under the layer of anger. Beneath the betrayal, and the shame, was relief. Relief he'd not turned away from me. A yearning to still be with him. A love that went deeper than just the flesh. "I still love you."

"And that's why I can live with it," he said, his face softening. "I wish there could have been another way. But…" He shrugged.

I could hear the truth in his words, just like I could feel the bond of our love getting stronger. How me having sex with another guy could make our love greater was a mystery, but I had no intention of letting him off the hook that easily. I needed to vent some more.

"You had no right to trick me like that. I waited twenty-three years to share my love and body with you. How could you force me into that kind of situation?" I asked, unable to hide my hurt. I knew, had the roles been reversed, I could never share Auric. He was mine, and I didn't share.

"I did what had to be done because I love you. Your wellbeing and safety trump petty feelings of jealousy. You could sleep with a thousand men, and I would still love you. It's not your fault that your power has special needs. I would rather you share your body to stay alive than to foolishly abstain and die. I couldn't live without you, Muriel."

"I won't share you, Auric."

"I know. And I'd have preferred not to share you either, but part of loving you means I need to understand and support what you need, including what your magic needs. Now are you done being pissed at me?"

"No." My lower lip jutted in a pout.

"Too bad." He crossed the short distance between us and wrapped me in a bear hug. "I missed you."

"You were gone one day."

"So? I still missed you."

I wanted to hold on to my anger, but it slipped away like a fish caught in bare hands. Why was I trying to push Auric away? Even though I'd slept with another man, he still loved me.

*He still wants me.*

I lifted my face and closed my eyes when

his lips came down possessively on mine.

When he let me up for air several minutes later, I had to ask. "So did David call you as soon as the dirty deed was done? Or were you watching?" Had we had an audience the entire time? Had Auric stroked himself as David thrust into my body?

He at least had the grace to look sheepish. "He called while you were in the shower. He also told me you wouldn't kiss him. Thank you."

I blushed; I couldn't help it. He looked so happy I'd reserved that treat for him.

"So, now what?" I asked.

"Now we plan an orgy."

I slammed my foot down on his insole, and he sucked in a breath. "Just kidding," he wheezed. "We'll take this slow, but Muriel, we can't wait too long. I got a report this afternoon that souls might be disappearing in Hell again. We think Azazel's master is planning something. We need to be ready."

I trembled, and my vision blurred for a second as the fear flooded me. Auric held me tightly while the attack passed.

We couldn't wait any longer, especially not if the hooded one was making a move. And I had to be strong enough to fight him. Which meant...

"I want this curse out of my head," I

whispered. "Let's do it now. Tonight." Before I chickened out.

"Sit down and wait for me. I'll grab David in the bar and tell him to meet us back at the loft." Another hard kiss and Auric left me with my thoughts—part excitement, part curiosity. How did a threesome work? Was I ready?

Ready or not, tonight had to be the night. If the master had returned with some nefarious plot in mind, then I needed to be able to face him without pissing my pants.

Auric returned. "It's a go."

I couldn't help a flutter of excitement.

Leaving by the side entrance, Auric peered around for watching eyes before he unfurled his beautiful shadow wings. Charcoal gray in color, they jutted from his back. They were like the thinnest gossamer to touch, almost ephemeral in presence. But their fragile appearance hid great strength.

Auric swept me off my feet before bounding into the air and letting his wings pump. With bold strokes, he lifted us from the ground, higher and higher until we soared above the city, just another shadow in the night sky.

I had twined my arms tightly around his neck because, while I did trust him to hold me, I still feared gravity. Since he did all the work, it left me free to do other things like nibble on his chin and neck. When that didn't get me a reaction, I wiggled a hand between our bodies and squeezed him.

Auric sucked in a breath. "What are you doing?"

"Playing."

"You need to stop, or you're going to make us crash."

"Am I distracting you?" I teased, sliding my hand into his pants to curl around his partially stiff cock. I stroked his velvety skin, enjoying the way he expanded in my hand and how his breathing grew ragged.

Too soon we arrived at the fire escape for the loft, and he bundled me inside, his hands ripping at my clothes until I stood nude before him.

"You are so fucking beautiful," he growled.

"Show me." I ran to the bed and hopped on.

For the moment we were still alone, as David hadn't arrived yet. With a coy smile and a crooked finger, I beckoned Auric, who stripped before taking long strides to meet me. He fell on me, a ravenous beast with seeking, hot lips. I met his hungry kisses and added in some sinuous tongue.

We rolled on the bed, seeking to

dominate the other and enjoying the feel of our naked skin rubbing together. The wrestling stopped when I found myself on the bottom while a very erect Auric pinned me. He held my hands above my head, and his green eyes smoldered. I licked my lips.

The smile he shot me was pure wickedness. It caught my breath.

He lowered his head to suck on my erect nipple. I moaned and tried to pull my hands free to grab his head, but he held them, a prisoner to his teasing. His hot mouth swirled on the erect nub, and I squirmed, enjoying the sensation. But while he tortured one breast, the other languished.

"Suck the other one," I demanded, and I was obeyed, just not in the way I expected.

A gasp escaped me as another set of warm lips latched onto my other breast.

Shocked, I opened my eyes to see David had joined the fray, his blond head alongside Auric's ebony one. Side by side, they teased my nipples with their mouths and tongues. So different in technique, so freaking hot. The view of them both pleasing me—not to mention the feel of it—only served to increase my arousal.

My body tingled from head to toe as all my senses awakened. Could I handle this much pleasure? Could I—

As if sensing my wavering attention, I felt almost simultaneous nips that made me cry out. I closed my eyes again and allowed myself to become lost in the sensation of their dual oral assault.

Auric had slid to the side but kept one leg thrown over my thigh. Like a reflecting mirror, David snuggled closer to my other side and put his leg over mine as well. Auric pulled one hand down from where it held mine prisoner, but one of David's hands took its place.

Their dominant takeover of my body made me squirm and pant. My pussy throbbed in anticipation, slick with my juices. They must have read my mind—or smelled my arousal—because their free hands pulled my thighs apart.

A callused hand stroked one inner thigh while a smooth, long-fingered one stroked the other. Like a synchronized dance, their fingers both sought the wetness of my sex. Two fingers from each man slid in and stretched me. With each touch, kiss, lick, stroke, I felt my power building. My inner reservoir of magic swelled. Overflowed.

I cried out, the electrical rush flooding my senses already so powerful I couldn't imagine holding more magic. But to my shock, my inner well kept expanding, and I floated on a powerful esoteric high that was enhanced by the sensual pleasure of my body.

At that point, I couldn't have said who was where, doing what. My eyes were closed as I lost myself in the moment. I shivered as a body slid between my legs, pushing them apart, exposing me. Warm breath fluttered against my damp sex. I quivered then cried out as a questing tongue slid across my clit.

When lips tugged at my swollen button, I bucked and would have cried out, but the sound was muffled by a hard cock, my mouth filled by Auric's shaft, whose size and shape I knew well. I lavished attention on his dick, sliding my lips over the taut skin as he fucked my mouth with his hard length. His fingers twined in my hair, controlling me and exciting me as he pulsed against my tongue, forcing me to deep throat him. How I loved it.

Between my thighs, my pussy trembled, wet and swollen. David's tongue flicked my clit, quickly making my hips twitch and writhe. I longed for him to put his fingers inside me, but he tortured me orally instead, stopping his attention to my swollen button, only to run a long, wet tongue against my quivering sex.

I wanted to plead for them to fuck me and make me come. I wanted to scream with the pleasure of it. The mind-blowing, pussy-drenching euphoria of having so much sexual attention lavished on me was almost too much. With my mouth full, all I could was hum and moan.

Again, as if choreographed, I found myself suddenly on my hands and knees, Auric's callused hands on my waist, the familiar thick head of his cock nudging my moist lips. I thrust my bottom back against him, and he responded by thrusting deep, stretching my slick pussy.

Squirming movement under me made me open my eyes, and I saw David positioning himself in a sixty-nine position under me, his cock poking me in the chin.

Auric pounded me fast and hard. I opened my mouth to cry out with the pleasure of it, but a hand on the back of my head pushed me down, and I got the hint. I took David's cock in my mouth, not as thick as Auric so I had no difficulty working it in and out of my mouth. I almost bit his shaft, though, when David wrapped his arms around my thighs and pulled his face up and, using that long tongue of his, licked me. He began flicking his tongue against my clit in time with Auric's thrusts.

How Auric managed to piston me while David licked me at the same time I didn't know or care because it felt so fucking good.

I quickly found myself climaxing, my cry muffled around the shaft in my mouth. But my pleasure didn't stop as Auric thrust in and out of me faster, my quivering pussy squeezing him tightly until, with a hoarse cry, his cock jerked and shot warm semen inside me.

And still they weren't done. I found myself flipped onto my back and my legs pushed up. David took his turn now between my thighs, something I caught only a glimpse of before Auric captured my lips and, with a rough hand, squeezed my breast. My hips were lifted up off the bed, my legs dangling over David's shoulders so he could fuck me deep. His long cock ended up in just the right position to stroke my G-spot.

I whimpered against Auric's lips, but torturer that he is, he slid a hand down and rubbed my clit while swallowing my cries with his mouth. With a scream, I came again, biting Auric's lip in my wild abandon. David prepared to withdraw on the brink of his own pleasure, but Auric growled, "Stay."

And so David plunged deep, my trembling sex welcoming him back. Auric hadn't stopped rubbing my clit, and to my intense shock, I found myself shuddering in the grips of yet another orgasm. Auric caught my cry with his lips, but I heard David shout as he exploded inside me, a molten stream of cum.

The powerful energy of his orgasm, along

with the ones that preceded it, sent my magic levels shooting higher than they'd ever gone before. I didn't just overflow with it. I exploded!

I writhed as if on fire. The surplus of magic raced through my body, looking for an outlet, burning a path wherever it went. It found the darkness pulsing in my head. Found that obscene impurity.

My magic attacked the spell that caged me. It cleansed me, burning it away.

I bucked and screamed as my mind caught on fire. Images flashed—of the cowled figure, myself whimpering... Faster and faster, scenes whipped by until, with an explosion of white light behind my eyelids, the geas of fear disintegrated.

Immediate relief flooded me, a tension I'd not realized was there easing. *My mind belongs to me again.*

The difference was so blatant that I cursed myself for not realizing just how badly the spell had affected me.

Overwhelmed, I fought to regain my breathing. The boys lay slumped on either side of me, breathing just as heavily.

I turned my head and faced Auric, his green eyes tender and loving. "Are you okay?" he asked.

I nodded and then smiled. Free of fear,

not to mention pleasantly sore, I'd never felt better. "The spell is gone, but I used up all my magic burning it out."

Auric's face split into a grin. "Are you trying to tell us something?"

The jerk, he intended to make me spell it out. My confidence and bravery completely restored, I impishly trailed a finger down both their chests, my hand finding and stroking their velvety shafts. To my immense, insatiable glee, they both immediately hardened. "So when's round two?"

Apparently, right away. Lucky me.

# CHAPTER TWELVE

Auric broached the subject of David moving in while I ate breakfast—which included many strips of bacon.

Coffee spewed all over the kitchen island, and I glared at Auric as he wiped it up.

"Excuse me?" My polite words held a strong hint of ice.

"I said I think David should move in with us."

Having not suffered from a nightmare for the first time in a month, I'd woken in a fabulous mood, not to mention a sated one. Damn, but our threesome of the previous night had charged my magical batteries as well as wiped the heavy pall of fear from my psyche. But with Auric's suggestion, I lost my happy glow.

"The geas on me is gone. Why the fuck would he move in?" I asked and not very nicely.

To those wondering, David had thankfully been gone when I woke up, which was good because it meant I didn't have to avoid eye contact, worrying about blushing. But it didn't mean I didn't fantasize. In the light of day, my actions of the previous night seemed depraved and slutty, but I also couldn't deny I had immensely enjoyed it, and a part of me wanted to do it again.

The fact that I craved it frightened me. But I was even more frightened of Auric's proposal. Was this his way of testing to see if things had changed between us? If I said yes to David moving in, would Auric take it as a sign I didn't love him enough?

"There're several reasons why it makes sense for him to move in. For one thing, you're still in danger."

"Welcome to my life."

"Exactly. Which leads me to reason number two. What if I'm not here and you need a magical boost?"

"Then I wait for you to come back." Even I knew the answer was lame. We'd seen what happened when I expended too much.

"Don't be an idiot. And don't let pride make you deny what you need."

Not pride, love. But there wouldn't be much of me to love if I died because I wouldn't have sex with someone, and someone Auric was shoving in my face—literally. I'd not forgotten how he made me suck David's cock. The erotic reminder didn't help my feeble argument.

What argument? Auric was right, and I

was being stubborn. "Fine. David can be a sex surrogate when you're gone. Happy? But that doesn't mean he needs to move in." I enjoyed sharing the loft with Auric, and while I liked David, I didn't want him here all the time. What would happen to alone time for me and Auric?

However, Auric remained adamant. "I want him close at hand."

"Why, so we can have threesomes every night? Am I not enough for you anymore?" I spoke bitterly, but only because the thought of the pleasure made me wet.

He sighed, pinching the bridge of his nose. "David moving in doesn't mean threesomes every night. What it means is I won't be putting off missions because I'm worried about you. It means us all being together and ready for the next time that hooded bastard or another wanna-be makes a move. It means giving David a sense of belonging so he doesn't feel used."

His words hit me hard, and I almost reeled back. "You've been turning down missions?" Never mind that he never spoke of what exactly these missions entailed, I knew how important they were to him.

He just nodded.

"Because of me?" Fuck and double fuck. I loved that Auric's world revolved around me, but dammit, I didn't want him resenting me because he had to give up the things that made me love him.

"Just think about it, would you?" he asked.

And I did. I thought about it while I showered. I thought about it when Auric walked me to work. I still hadn't come to a decision when Bambi walked into the bar.

Once again, I dragged her from the common area to my office.

"I need your advice again," I said, pacing the small confines of my office.

"What is it this time, lamb?"

No point beating around the bush. "I had a threesome with David and Auric."

Bambi's mouth rounded in an O of surprise.

"Yes, I know—shocking." I waved my hands in agitation when she didn't speak. "But it wasn't because I wanted to. I had to."

"You had to have sex with two men?"

"Yeah. See, Dad's mages discovered I had some spell put on me that was giving me all those nightmares and stuff. In order to get rid of it, I needed sex, actually orgasms, a lot of them pretty much at once."

"I'll be damned. My baby sister is exploring her sexuality." Bambi giggled when I glared at her. "So what's the problem?" she asked. "Sounds to me like you've got your hands full and in a good way. That David is a hunk."

Yes he was, which wasn't helping at all.

"Problem is, Auric thinks David should move in."

"And you don't want to because?" she queried with an arched brow.

"Because it's not right. I love Auric. He's my consort. How the Hell are we supposed to be a couple if we've got another guy living with us? A guy, I might add, Auric expects me to fuck if he's not around for a power boost and to indulge in the occasional threesome if we really need to charge my batteries."

Bambi shrugged. "I still don't see your problem."

"A couple is two people, one man, one woman, unless you're bi that is. Not two men, one woman."

"Bullshit."

"How is it bullshit?"

Bambi leaned forward. "Because there is no one set of rules when it comes to relationships. Yes, monogamy works for some, just as threesomes and foursomes work for others. I'm surprised you're so close-minded about this."

"Are you calling me a prude?"

"Let me ask you this, did you enjoy it?"

Lying to my sister wasn't an option. "Yes."

"Does Auric still love you?"

"Yes."

"Then again, I don't see the problem."

But there was a problem. A whole bunch of them starting with, "What about poor David in this? How is he going to find himself a girlfriend"—*grrrr*—"if he's living with us and fucking me?"

"Why don't you ask him?"

My mouth snapped shut. Funny, in all the musing I'd done, that had never occurred to me. What did David think?

"Perhaps David is the one who asked Auric to move it. Maybe he's got feelings for you. Did you ever think of that?"

No, I hadn't, which meant even more turmoil in my mind. I frowned at Bambi. "You're really not helping me here."

"Listen, lamb, you want my advice, and here it is. I'm not saying if David moves in everything will be exactly the same. Of course it won't, but that doesn't mean it will automatically be bad. And you need to face facts. You are a princess of Hell with sex-based magic, and your consort is a man of the world who can't sit around to hold your fucking hand. You want alone time with Auric. You make some. Set some boundaries. Plan a date night. I'm sure, if you talk to them, you can come to some kind of arrangement you can all live with. I know Auric, lamb. He wouldn't suggest this if he didn't think it was necessary. And to be honest, if David comes to live with you, he won't be looking for a girlfriend. I've seen how he watches you. That boy is already in love with you. Now I know you don't care for him the same way you do Auric, but can you honestly say you don't care for him at all? That you wouldn't freak if you saw him with another girl now that you've slept with him?"

I opened my mouth to retort and then shut it again. The thought of David touching another woman... I saw red.

Oh, fuck me. I loved Auric with all my being, but I couldn't deny I cared for David.

I sat down on my couch with a heavy sigh. "When did my life get so complicated? Just a month ago I was a virgin who only had to worry about running out of double As for my vibrating rocket. Now I've got two lovers."

"My little sister is growing up," said Bambi with a laugh. "Don't look so glum. Do you know how many women would kill to be in your panties?" With a wave, she left me to my thoughts.

Once again, the world's biggest slut— Bambi took pride in this title and even had a trophy to prove it—had guided me through a life crisis.

It looked like I'd be getting a roommate. Not that I'd tell Auric right away. Let him work at me a bit more. I wanted to enjoy the little alone time we had left before my life changed again irrevocably.

And, hopefully, pleasurably.

# CHAPTER THIRTEEN

"Muriel!"

The panicked shout by my father startled me awake. Lifting my head from my pillow, I regarded my dad with annoyance, ready to blast him for disturbing my sleep until I noticed what he wore—a brilliant red parka and a tuque with a pompom, definitely not my father's usual Armani attire and very unusual given my dad hated the cold. So why was he bundled for snow and arctic temperatures?

At the first scent of brimstone, Auric had jumped out of bed and stood gloriously nude with his sword in hand, the metal one, not the flesh one. When he saw my dad, he sighed and crawled back under the covers.

"Dad, can't you ever call first?" I glared at him as I asked because his presence meant no morning nookie for me unless I got rid of him quickly.

"Why call when this is much quicker?" My father just couldn't—or should I say wouldn't?— grasp the concept of privacy and boundaries.

Auric snorted and flung an arm over his face, probably to hide a grin.

"Dad, you can't just pop in like that. I live with Auric now, and you have to start respecting our space. Now I want you to go now and call before you decide to just pop in."

"But this is an emergency. You said emergencies were okay." He looked so crestfallen that I sighed.

"Fine, what's so important that you couldn't knock?" *And it better be good*, I thought.

"Hell's frozen over!"

That caught my attention. Sitting up in the bed, I only barely remembered to grab the sheet and hold it over my naked bosom. "What did you say?" I had to have misheard.

"Hell has frozen over," my father repeated slowly through gritted teeth. "As in covered in a blanket of white. No heat. No fire. Frozen solid like a Popsicle."

Now my dad's outfit made sense. I absorbed this surprising news and then... I laughed. I roared. I giggled insanely.

"Muriel!" shouted my father. "I fail to see the humor."

I stopped gasping long enough to say. "Well, your outfit for one. I mean, Dad, really, a bright red parka? Couldn't you have found something a little more manly?"

My perplexed dad—evil lord of the pit—looked down at his crimson coat with matching red wooly mitts, the pompom on his hat dangling. "Who cares about my coat? Don't you grasp what Hell freezing over means?"

"Not really," I replied with a shrug. "You, Auric?"

"I think," Auric replied slowly, his face creased in thought, "that this might not be a laughing matter." He looked at my dad and asked, "Were they all documented?"

My father nodded his head. "Every single one. No one ever thought it would come to pass. But a promise made is a promise made."

Confusion made me scrunch up my face. I really hated it when I was the last to understand. "What are you both talking about?"

Auric explained it to me. "Everyone who's ever made a pledge using the term 'when Hell freezes over' is having to fulfill their promise."

"But they don't know Hell's frozen over. It's not like Dad's going to take out a full page ad and announce it to the world. Not to mention, if these folks weren't going to follow through on their promise before, why would they do it now?"

My father groaned. "I can't believe my own daughter doesn't grasp the gravity."

"Muriel," said Auric with a patience I

envied, "these pledges people made were all documented, and due to the high improbability involved, because of course Hell should have never frozen over, they are now being forced to fulfill those pledges."

"What? But that's insane. I mean the term 'when Hell freezes over' is used like a zillion times a day and is only used in the grossest of circumstances. It was never meant to be taken seriously." It was then the gravity of it finally struck, and I blanched. "Oh shit, this will get ugly." How many girls had told guys they'd sleep with them only when Hell froze over? How many ultimatums delivered with that promise? This was so bad.

"Finally, she gets it," my father shouted, rolling his eyes and flinging up his hands. "Now for the only good news. The magic is starting with the oldest entries first, and those people are already dead. So we have a little time before it hits the live ones and people start upholding their promises."

Which meant the world was about to see a wave of vile acts. "Wait a second. Why do you care?" I asked my dad. "As Satan, shouldn't you be cheering all the evil that's going to come of this?"

My father shook his head. "Aah, Muri. If we don't stop this, I'm going to be handing down punishments and dealing with paperwork for centuries. It will totally cut into my golf and wenching time."

Now I rolled my eyes. My father, the altruistic one.

"What do you want us to do?" asked Auric, getting out of bed again, this time to get dressed in warm, concealing clothes. What a shame.

"We need to get the flames of Hell burning again." My father said this as if it would be a simple matter. Somehow I didn't think a can of lighter fluid and a match would do the trick.

"Flames of Hell, right," I muttered. Then I finally had a light bulb moment, and I wanted to dance. Satana, princess of Hell, was back! "I know what the riddle means!" I exclaimed, bouncing on the bed.

My father and Auric both turned to face me with puzzled expressions. I laughed at them, proud I'd finally figured something out on my own before they had. "Hello. Azazel's warning, and I quote, 'when winter arrives, he'll be waiting for you by the furnace'."

"This is the work of the hooded one." Auric nodded at me with a proud smile that made me preen.

"I guess the next question is if this frozen Hell thing is a spell or something else. Have you noticed any souls missing?" I asked my father.

My father shrugged, looking tired. "There's always souls missing. Hell is kind of big in case you hadn't noticed. I've had my people tracking down the souls that have been reported as having disappeared, but it takes time. Although it definitely looks like some are permanently gone, just like last time."

"I guess the real question is, what do we do next?" said Auric.

"One thing is for sure. We have to do something soon before the magic starts claiming the promises of those still living. I'd like to kill the person who coined that stupid phrase. When Hell freezes over. What a stupid thing to say." My dad grumbled, his way of dealing with anxiety.

"Time to kick some hooded ass." Look at that, I didn't collapse in a quivering heap. I grinned at the proof that there was no more fear in me. "I need to get dressed. I've got a meeting that I don't intend to miss with a certain asshat." I couldn't wait to let the bastard in the robe meet the edge of my blade.

"I'd better call David and Christopher," said Auric. He walked away to grab his cell, and I looked at my dad.

"We're gonna fix this, Daddy."

For a moment, I thought I saw a glimmer of fear in my father's face. Satan, afraid?

Never.

"I have faith in you and your friends, Muri. And don't worry, this time you won't be fighting alone. I'm mobilizing my demonic forces as we speak."

I decided to not point out that, if Hell truly was as cold as he said, his demons would be close to useless. Like many animals on the mortal plane, extreme cold sent them into a hibernating mode. Hopefully my dad had enough mittens and parkas for all of them, or we'd be facing the hooded one by ourselves, which suited me just fine.

I had a score to settle.

# CHAPTER FOURTEEN

David arrived before Chris, and heat invaded my cheeks, probably because I couldn't help but mentally flash to a moment from the night before when he'd been fucking me and I'd looked up to see him, his muscled abs straining, his hips pumping...

Desire soaked my panties. David sniffed the air and grinned at me, a cocky smile so unlike his usual shyness that I found myself torn between slapping him for knowing I was horny and ripping off his clothes for a new round of sexual fun.

I did neither. Just turned my back and pretended interest in my boots. Ugly, practical things, but as Auric had assured me, they'd keep my feet warm, even if they had never made any fashion list.

Auric came out of the storage room, carrying down-filled jackets and threw them on the couch.

"Good, you're here," he said with a nod to David. "Christopher is gonna be another hour or so. That should give us enough time."

"Enough time for what?" I asked.

Two pairs of eyes, one blue, one green,

swiveled to look at me, the gleam in them unmistakable and arousing. Looking at both men standing there expectantly, I was suddenly struck by their startling contrast. One so fair and boyish looking, the other dark and dangerous. They both drew me and my magic. Heat coiled between my thighs.

"Hold on a second. This isn't the time to being getting down and doing the nasty. Hello, Hell has frozen over. Focus here." I licked my lips even as I spoke, my knees trembling and tummy swirling with excitement. I couldn't deny I wanted it, but I was determined to at least try and make it look like I didn't.

"Strip, Muriel," Auric ordered me.

"But—"

"Or I'll put you over my knee and spank you."

Damn, get naked and have a great time or refuse and also have a great time. Fuck, I loved my life.

But a sore ass might not be the most comfortable thing when facing true evil, so with a coy smile, I stripped. Why argue with what my body—and, I'd admit, even my mind—wanted.

Naked, I stood there proudly, displaying my lush curves and enjoying their smoky looks and the evident erections in their pants. I cupped my breasts, rolling my nipples between my fingers, loving the hungry look they got on their faces, as if they wanted to make me their main course. Quickly, both men shed their clothes, and the heat inside me grew at the sight of their naked, muscled bodies.

Auric approached me first. He dropped to his knees and, with his fingers gripping my thighs, spread my legs. David watched us, his hand on his cock, stroking it. As Auric's tongue found my wet pussy and licked, I found myself unable to look away from David and the long rod he pumped in his fist.

The flood of desire that raced through my body made my knees buckle, and I ended up sitting on the couch, Auric still between my legs, lapping at my moist core. David ended up on the couch beside me, his mouth latched onto my tit. I grabbed his shaft, jerking its velvety hot length. David bit down on my nipple, and I screamed, a sound I repeated when Auric shoved three fingers inside of me and stretched me, even as he kept flicking my clit with the tip of his tongue.

"Please," I begged, already mindless with pleasure.

"Tell me what you want," growled Auric.

"Fuck me." I panted. "Make me come."

And like my words had been what they waited for, I found myself on my knees on the couch, my arms braced on the armrest. A slim rod entered my pussy from behind and started a rhythm, one that Auric joined when he shoved his cock between my lips. Fingers laced in my hair, Auric fucked my mouth, forcing me to take his long length, grunting as I sucked.

A sharp, stinging slap on my ass made me squeal around the shaft in my mouth, but both men seemed to enjoy it, for they moved even faster. The grip in my hair got tighter, painfully so, but that only enhanced my pleasure and sent me over the edge. I orgasmed hard, my pelvic muscles spasming around David's prick.

More slaps sounded out, making my ass cheeks throb pleasantly and, to my even greater shock, making another orgasm erupt. With synchronized bellows, both of my lovers came.

I glowed and fairly burst with magic after that explosive sexual bout. I wanted to bask for a moment in the pleasure because I knew once I opened my eyes it would be time to go kill the hooded one.

A slap on my ass made me squeak, "Hey. Enough already."

"Stop daydreaming and get dressed," Auric commanded.

"You're bossy."

"And you love it."

I did.

In short order, we'd piled on the warm layers. Christopher arrived, big staff in hand—his wooden magic one, not his fleshy one. With the crew gathered, it wasn't long before we were stepping through the portal Auric called.

I walked from the chilly rift into an even chillier wonderland.

Hell looked kind of pretty covered in a pristine coat of white snow. Instead of ash trickling from the sky, fluffy snowflakes drifted down. Everywhere I looked I could see demons bundled in layers and the souls of the damned tobogganing and throwing snowballs, and just having a good time. I liked it.

It wasn't hard to spot my father. That bright red jacket of his stood out. I made my way to his side and said, "You know what, Dad? This is actually a good look for Hell."

My father just glared at me, his teeth chattering, which I had to admit took away a lot from the look.

The imp inside me, unable to resist, teased, "Hey, I bet if we took a video of this and posted it on HellTube we could crash their servers." That earned me another dirty look, which made me laugh, that was until a snowball hit me upside the head.

Turning, I saw Auric grinning from ear to ear.

"You are so dead." I scooped up some of the white stuff and threw it back. Auric ducked, and I hit David in the back of the head instead. I giggled when he turned around, but then squealed when he came racing across the snow at me. I took off running, not making it far before a hard body tackled me into a soft drift. A body that tumbled quickly off mine when somebody else dove into it.

Rolling over, I saw David and Auric wrestling in the snow, each trying to snow job the other. I laughed breathlessly and lay on my back. Spreading my arms and legs back and forth, I made a snow angel. Surely a first for Hell.

A shadow fell over me, and I peered into my father's exasperated face.

"And to think all our hopes rest on you," he muttered, shaking his head.

I held out a hand, and my father, still superbly strong for his age, yanked me to my feet.

"You mean I get to save the day?" I didn't bother to hide my excited eagerness. Now that the oppressive weight of that fear spell was gone, I felt ready to take on anything.

"If you children are done playing," my dad said with a pointed look at David and Auric as they came jogging up, "then perhaps we can go speak to the mages and see if they have any answers for us."

Christopher, who'd stood by and watched our snow play, just shook his head. Spoilsport.

Dad, head held high and trying to look every inch the lord of lies and damnation—and failing in his fire engine red parka—trudged through the thick snow, his grumblings too low to make out.

Auric and David positioned themselves on either side of me, and to my pleasure, each held my hand. I could see Chris looking at us sideways, but he said not a word.

I wondered how much Auric had told him. He and Chris were close friends, almost as close as he and David. It made me wonder why he'd chosen David instead of Chris to complete our ménage. Did he not trust Chris as much? Did Chris find the whole three-way thing gross? Or even more unlikely, did Chris not find me attractive?

Nah. But I added that question to my growing list that I planned to eventually ask Auric when things got back to normal, well as normal as things could get with us planning to live with another guy and my nympho magic.

Entering the palace, we shook the snow from our clothes and followed my dad into his war room, a vast space with maps on every wall, magical maps that had blinking lights.

His wrinkled mages were already stationed around the war table, and the guys joined them. Me, I wandered over to spy on the wall and ogle the maps that represented each of the circles of Hell. Bright red lights kept popping up on the detailed grids as I looked at them.

"What are the red lights?" I asked, turning from the wall to see the boys huddled over something on the immense table.

"Confirmed missing souls," replied my father, not even looking up.

I faced the maps again, and my stomach sank. The red lights kept appearing, their number staggering, each one a soul that would never live again. It made me more determined than ever to stop Azazel and his hooded master. I would avenge the souls of those who'd been taken.

Go, princess of Hell! I was my own cheering squad.

My father, the guys, and the three prune faces bored me with their talk of tactics. I just wanted to be pointed in a direction so I could find something to kill.

Leaving the war room, I wandered down the hall until I ended up in the rock garden, now covered in a sheet of white.

It seemed like forever since I'd run here, trying to fight what my body and magic needed me to do. And now look at me. Indulging in threesomes at the drop of a pair of pants. At least Auric seemed happy with the arrangement, but I'd forsake my magic in a moment if he wasn't.

A sound from behind saw me pulling my Hell sword from the scabbard at my side and whirling, its red pointed tip inches from the throat of a minor demon that had entered the garden.

The ugly beast with his stubby horns swallowed and said not a word, just lifted a box it held in two hands toward me.

"A present? For me?" Not being the trusting type, I kept my sword in one hand while reaching for the gift with the other. The minor demon, seeing I had the package in hand, immediately scurried off.

How odd to receive a gift. It wasn't even my birthday. I eyed the white box with its pretty red bow and wondered who it was from. I didn't see a card. But a present was a present.

Sheathing my sword, I tore open the package and ripped apart the tissue paper. When I beheld the contents, a red rage descended over me.

It contained a blood-covered brassiere and a lock of hair that I recognized. A note accompanied the items, and I scanned it, my fury growing.

*I have your sister, but the person I really want is you. The question is do you care for your sister as much as your lover? Will you trade your life for hers? Or will she die painfully, knowing her favorite little sister has forsaken her? Will you let her die cursing your name? I await you by the furnace. Come alone, or I will make her die slowly, one scream at a time.*

"Fuck! Fuck! Fuck!" I paced and kicked at the snow angrily. That hooded prick had taken my sister. I already knew I would go after her. I couldn't stay here and do nothing. A surrogate mother, Bambi had always been there for me, bandaging my cuts, teaching me to wear makeup, how to flirt, the best way to kick a man in the balls. She'd done so much for me. Now it was my turn to do something for her.

The problem, though, was, did I tell the boys or not? I loved my father, but I feared he'd sacrifice my sister to keep me safe. He didn't feel the same way about my succubi sisters as he did me, something I didn't quite understand. If I were even more honest, Auric and David would probably side with him. Not many beings relegated importance to succubi. I did though.

*Bambi matters.*

For that reason alone, I'd go, even if I had to face the wanna-be master alone. I wondered if he knew yet that the magical geas on my mind had been destroyed. If he didn't, I could use that to my advantage.

Determined, I strutted from the rock garden and headed for the front doors. I should have known I wouldn't be able to sneak out of the palace. I'd almost reached the entrance when Auric barked in a commanding tone, "And just where do you think you're going, woman?"

Oops. Caught. But I wouldn't cower, nor would I back down.

Tilting my chin stubbornly, I turned to face stormy green eyes. "Going to take care of business."

"Without telling me first?"

"He's got Bambi."

"And?" Auric stalked toward me, his body bristling with anger. "Are you trying to tell me you were just going to waltz out of here, alone, to confront the hooded fellow?"

"That was the plan, yes." I braced myself for the storm.

"Are you out of your fucking mind?" he shouted.

"She's my sister. I won't let him kill her," I yelled back and stood toe to toe with him.

"Of course we won't let Bambi die."

"What?" His answer took me aback.

"Did you really think I'd be callous enough to leave your sister to die? I'd never do that. Ever. What I do object to is you going off like some idiot on your own."

"I'm not an idiot," I grumbled, but my eyes dropped and my cheeks flushed red at his chastisement.

Strong arms wrapped around me, and his lips kissed my temple softly. "No, you're not. You're wonderful and loving and brave. But you forgot one thing."

I melted at wonderful. "What did I forget?"

"You don't have to do this alone."

He didn't know about the note. "He'll kill her if I show up with you guys."

"He'll kill us all if he gets his hands on you."

Good point. Of course I had no intention of letting him capture me, so it was also a moot point.

"Fine, smartass. Since you seem to have it all worked out, what's your plan then?" I asked. I expected him to bluster, but as usual, Auric had stayed one step ahead of me.

"While you were off deciding to save Hell all by yourself, I learned some interesting things."

"Like?"

"Like you can draw magic from David and me, even if we're not doing the naked tango."

That caught my attention. "How?"

"Nefertiti, the mage who examined you before, says it's not quite as effective as the actual act itself, but if there's a bond between us, and we're aroused and within sight, you can pull on that arousal to fuel your magic."

"Let me get this straight. You want me to be horny going into battle and stay horny so I'll have more magic?"

Auric nodded. I laughed and laughed some more, my mirth so strong it brought tears to my eyes.

"What's so funny?" asked David, who had joined us.

"I told Muriel about the new aspect to her magic that we just discovered."

"Oh," replied David.

I wheezed, trying to control my giggles.

*Smack!*

The cracking slap on my ass cheek sobered me up quickly, and I stood up, glaring at Auric and David, who regarded me innocently. Rubbing my posterior, I scowled at them both.

Chris chose that moment to come sauntering up. "I see you stopped her. Have you briefed her on the plan so we can get this show on the road?"

"Plan?" I seesawed my gaze between the guys. "What plan?"

"We know the hooded one is waiting by the furnace, right?" Auric spoke up. "What he and Azazel probably don't know is there are actually two ways to get to the furnace."

"Since when?" I asked. My father had never told me about that.

"Your dad only found out about it just now from Nefertiti. She found it when scrying the area. Says it's been there a long time, hidden by the flames that are usually there. Using this secret entrance will give us an advantage."

I now wished I'd stayed for the meeting. Apparently it had been more interesting than I'd expected.

"Muriel, you'll approach the furnace from the main entrance while David and I sneak into the hidden rear one. Chris will follow you after a certain interval to help guard your rear. Your father will stay here with the army and, at our signal, will open a portal right outside the furnace that will launch his soldiers into the fray."

That made sense. My father alone possessed the power needed to open a portal the size and duration needed to get an army through. But I bet he hated being left behind. He did so enjoy a good fight.

"Sounds good. Let's go." My blood pumped in anticipation, eager for action.

"Not quite yet. Chris, we'll just be a few minutes."

"What? Why aren't we leaving?" Auric grabbed me by the hand and dragged me off into a chamber adjoining the main hall, a parlor of sorts for waiting visitors. David followed and closed the double doors.

"We just need to do one more thing before we go through a portal and kick some ass."

I eyed them suspiciously. "I'm already full up on magic, so you can forget about having sex. Let's go save Bambi."

"Oh, I know you're full," said Auric with a naughty gleam in his eye. "We just need to make sure you're titillated enough to draw some more if you need it."

I backed up a step as Auric stalked me, sexual intent in his eyes. I hit something hard, and arms wrapped around my waist. David nuzzled my ear and whispered, "This will only take a few minutes." Then he licked the shell of my ear before biting my earlobe and making my knees sag.

Auric stood in front of me, his green eyes smoldering with lust. "Cup me, baby," he growled. "Feel how much I want you."

I couldn't stop myself from obeying. Placing my hand over his groin, I sighed at how hard he was. I squeezed him, and he groaned. David, eager to not be left out, ground his own erection against the crack of my ass. He also slid his hands up from my waist to cup and squeeze my tits.

My head fell back as Auric also placed his hands on me, his callused thumbs lifting my shirt and stroking the soft skin at my waist. A pressure against my crotch followed by warmth had me mewling as Auric, who had dropped to his knees, teased me with his mouth over the fabric of my pants.

Desire roared through me, my juices soaking through the fabric of my panties and slacks. I heard Auric grunt, his mouth so hot against me. David flicked my nipples through the fabric of my shirt, sensitizing my nubs, even as he kept rubbing himself against my backside.

Lost in a maelstrom of sensation, I heard myself pleading. "Fuck me. Now. Please."

Instead, they both moved away from me, their breathing heavy, their cocks straining the material of their jeans.

Auric said not a word as he zipped my coat up, but he did kiss me, a hard, bruising kiss that made me grab his hair and pull.

Untangling my hands from him, he set me back. His voice unsteady, he said, "Let's go kill the bad guy, and when we're done, if you're a good girl, I am going to fuck you so hard. I am going to pound you until you see stars. Then I'm going to fuck you some more."

"And while he's fucking you," David said from behind me, "you're going to be gagging on my shaft until I cream you."

I shuddered, and I was pretty sure I had a mini orgasm just with their words.

"What are we waiting for?" I demanded impatiently, pushing past them. "Let's get this show on the road." So I could put out the fire they'd started in my crotch.

Nothing like incentive to get a girl going.

# CHAPTER FIFTEEN

Auric sketched the portal that would deposit me not far from the mountain housing the furnace. With one last kiss from my fallen angel, I stepped through the glowing interdimensional rift into a white blizzard.

Great.

I slogged through the sticky flakes that I no longer found so pretty. In the distance, through blustery gusts, I could see a stone wall of black, and while I couldn't spot it yet, I knew at its base there was a crevice that led to the furnace itself.

No one knew the origins of Hell's inferno; it had always been. The closest comparison was a gigantic hearth that made Hell hot and dry, not to mention sifted ash down constantly.

Pit scientists speculated the flames came from a volcano buried deep under the crust of Hell. No one knew for sure. Whatever the source, it was damned hot!

I'd once asked my father what made it burn during a visit to the inferno when much younger, and my father had replied the sins of the world were the fuel that fed its fire. It made one wonder just where the sins were going now that they weren't getting roasted like marshmallows. I also wondered how the heck I'd get the fire going again. If I killed the hooded one, would the spell vanish, lighting the furnace up again? Or would I have to do magic of my own?

Hopefully I'd find the answer when the time came.

After much cursing and crossing skiing off my bucket list, I reached the opening in the rock wall and I slipped inside, shivering from the cold.

The heat of my arousal had long dissipated. Auric's plan to make me horny had failed against the elements. Did I worry about it? Not really. I was a cocky bitch. This wouldn't be the first time I winged it—and won.

The quiet in the roughly hewn tunnel made the hair on my body bristle. I could sense power ahead of me. Great power. The wanna-be master, my tormentor, had already arrived.

Chattering teeth or not, I knew I couldn't fight wearing the thick parka and mitts. I shed the heavy clothing and drew my Hell blade. Instantly the flames came to life inside the red metal. It also radiated a bit of heat, just not enough to stop my shivering.

With nipples protruding from the cold, and a lot of attitude, I sashayed down the tunnel into the furnace room. No point in delaying.

The cowled one stood in front of the open maw that used to house the flames of Hades. A ball of light hung above it, faintly illuminating the area around it. Azazel, his demonic black face stretched in a toothy grin, stood beside his hooded master, and lying at their feet, in a huddled ball of misery, I saw Bambi.

My sister lifted her bloodied face, and for a moment, I saw hope in her eyes then loving resignation. "You shouldn't have come, lamb," she croaked. "Run. Run before it's too late."

Even now, my sister tried to protect me.

"Silence, bitch!" Azazel kicked her in the side, and Bambi fell face first onto the hard floor. She didn't move, but I growled.

Rage filled me, warm and welcome, making my body tingle in expectation. I'd originally planned to fake being under the hooded one's spell, but without the geas of fear, I discovered I couldn't pretend to be scared. On the contrary, I wanted, make that needed, to inspire fear.

I was, after all, Satana Muriel Baphomet, misbegotten daughter of Lucifer, princess of

Hell, and no one fucked with me or my family.

Something of my resolve must have shown on my face. Perhaps the flames I'd inherited from my father lit my eyes. Perhaps it was the sword I brandished menacingly or the fact that I pulled my lips back and grinned ferally at them.

I also glowed with power. My magical reservoir bulged, anxious for me to unleash it, and my hair danced in a static mess around my head as I stalked toward them, the gleaming red of my blade swinging hypnotically back and forth.

Azazel's eyes widened for a moment, but at a movement from the cowled figure, he straightened his spine and spat, "Stop moving or your sister dies."

I just smiled wider and tsked him much like I would a naughty child. "Touch another hair on her head and I will make you scream for an eternity instead of killing you quickly."

Stupid demon, he didn't run, even though I could see from his expression that he heard the truth in my words.

Funny, my father hated the truth, but personally, I'd always found it rather effective, its solid ring inspiring more fear than any lie could.

A whisper of power touched me, like a faint voice. I could hear it calling to the spell that used to reside in my mind.

*Fear me,* it chanted.

I trembled for a tenth of a second as that insidious ghostly touch on my psyche tried to wake the curse it had placed there.

Not happening. I feared nothing. I squashed the questing tendril and lashed back—with ridicule.

"Oops," I laughed. "Looking for your spell, are you? Hate to break it to you, but it's gone. Burned to a crisp. Kind of like what I intend to do to you. Unless you'd prefer I slowly slice you into pieces." Choices, choices. Even I didn't know which one I preferred.

"Get her," screeched the hooded one, finally losing his calm demeanor.

Azazel took one uncertain step forward, and I braced myself, my legs loosely bent. I beckoned him, but he hesitated, and I wondered at this until I heard the scuffing sounds of movement behind me.

"Foolish bitch. You may have left your bodyguards behind, but we came prepared," Azazel taunted.

The sound of a lot of shuffling feet didn't move the smile from my face. "Did I? Look again, asshole." Because floating down from the ceiling, his grey wings spread wide, was my very own angel, and he looked deliciously fierce.

Seeing the battle light in his eyes brought my lust back with a vengeance. As adrenaline and magic coursed through my veins, I twirled my sword, let out a battle cry, and charged.

Nothing like a good, loud yell to get the fighting started.

Azazel snarled and would have sprung at me if a big blond bundle of fur hadn't tackled him. Spitting and slashing, David, my giant kitty, had also arrived.

How nice to have lovers I could depend on. And reward later.

Auric landed beside me and pulled out his holy blade, its shining steel making me faintly ill. After all, his sword's purpose was to destroy evil things, and as Lucifer's daughter, I kind of fell into that category.

"Get your sister," Auric ordered. "I've got your back."

A quick glance behind me showed a wave of demons advancing in a line, their fangs dripping in excitement. "Are you sure?" I asked, utterly torn.

"Your father's forces are arriving as we speak. Now go. Do me proud, and I'll lick you until you come on my tongue later."

With that kind of encouragement, I ran for my sister, still prone on the ground.

What of the hooded one?

My eyes glanced at him and noted he

seemed to be doing something. But what? I could sense power coiling, but couldn't discern the purpose. Whatever it was, it wouldn't bode well. I had to stop it.

Screaming a war cry that would have made an Amazon proud, I dashed at him, the point of my sword leading the way. The robed one unfortunately moved before I skewered him, but at least I'd disrupted his spell.

I stood over my sister's body and hissed at the wanna-be master. Sometimes there were no words that would do.

The stupid bastard didn't even flinch like any other normal being would have.

Between my feet, Bambi stirred.

"Can you move?" I asked, keeping an eye on the hooded one, who once again had dropped into a trance, pulling at tendrils of power.

"I'll try," she gasped.

Even as she tried to get to her knees, a thundering crash and a flash of light made us turn to look toward the entrance to the furnace room. Holding a magical staff, Chris had arrived and, using raw magic, forced a path between the ranks of demons. He strode through his cleared opening, reinforcements from my father following him and joining the battle. Yay for the good, or should I say bad, guys.

In a moment, Chris had arrived at my side and scooped my sister. I gave him a nod of thanks and then turned to look for the hooded one. For a moment, I couldn't find the bastard, and then a shadow of movement caught my eye.

"Leaving the party already?" I said, strutting toward him. "But we haven't even gotten to the main event. Your death."

"Foolish girl child thinking you can stand against me." The robed one straightened, and a whirlpool of power swirled unseen around it.

Not so good.

In a moment of déjà vu, the cowled being approached me, hand outstretched. A faint remembrance of fear and pain shivered through me. I drew on my magic and lit a fire in my mind to keep its shadowy thoughts at bay. But he pushed hard against my psychic shield, doing his best to drain my magic.

"Fight me, damn it!" I cried. I took a step toward it, determined to decapitate it, but my legs moved sluggishly, as if mired in mud.

I let out a frustrated growl. Stubbornness should have been my middle name because, hard or not, I pushed against the inertia, gaining inches. The robed one was almost within reach of my sword.

"Satana," it whispered, its voice low and melodious. Male or female, I still couldn't tell, but I could feel the power emanating from it. A shitload of power and all aimed at me. And stupidly, I'd come too close to it and found myself wrapped in tendrils of its magic.

Swinging my sword did not cut the magical ties that tried to bind me, and the being chuckled, moving toward me now, hand outstretched, looking to touch.

For a moment, panic rose in my gorge.

Not again!

Then I found myself saved from a most unexpected source. Azazel. Bleeding and stumbling, trying to back away from the panther that stalked him, he bumped into his master, disrupting the spell that shackled me.

And that distraction allowed my men to reinforce me—my fallen angel on one side and my big, bad kitty on the other. Pity, nobody had a camera. It would have made a wicked picture for sure.

"Use us," whispered Auric, followed by a nudge on my other side by David's big, blond head. It occurred to me I was wasting time here with this cowardly being who wouldn't even show its face, time that could be spent at home naked in a three-way pretzel. And just like that, my lust roared back through me, and I drew on the magic I could somehow sense filtering from my lovers beside me.

Men I intended to lick every inch of later.

As if he read my mind, Auric growled. "I'm going to do more than lick you, woman. Let's finish this."

Energized, I smiled, teeth bared and feral. I knew the moment my eyes lit up with the flames of Hell because the one who would call himself master took a step back.

I could feel him send out a tendril of power at me.

*Don't move,* it coaxed.

I batted it down with my own energy and stalked forward, swinging my Hell sword.

Like a mouse who had suddenly caught the scent of a predator, the hooded one tried to scurry away. Not fucking likely.

"Tell me your name," I demanded, grabbing a hold of its loose robe, the material soft as silk. I could feel the being still trying to control me, but I guessed the boys were getting off sexually on my power trip because the magic flowing into me increased, and I even felt a new flavor join in, darker magic, cold with a hint of the grave. I couldn't have said who it belonged to, nor did I care. I inhaled it. And used it.

Drunk on power, I laughed at the robed one's feeble attempt to control my mind. "Enough!" I roared. I put some force into that request, my voice suddenly booming, and the battle that raged behind us, a battle I had blocked out until now, suddenly stopped. Silence reigned. "Tell me your name!" I commanded.

Fear emanated from the one in my grip.

Delicious.

"Tell me who you are," I whispered, my power twining insidiously with the words and bringing the cowled one trembling to his knees. I loved the reversal of roles.

I heard it croak something faintly.

"I didn't hear you. Tell me your name."

"Gabriel."

Kind of anticlimactic. "Pull off your hood." Damn, but I liked being in the driver seat and giving the commands.

The pale slender hands that been the centerpiece of my nightmares for so long trembled as they reached to grasp the edge of the hood and pushed it back.

An androgynous face stared back at me with only the squareness of the chin indicating it was male. Beautifully pure skin of the finest white marble and a gaze so serene that I wondered what race he belonged to. And also how something that looked so pretty could be so evil.

I stared, trying to make sense of this being, but the answer came from Auric who exclaimed, "You? You're the one behind this?"

"You know him?"

"Fucking right I do. Say hello to Gabriel, one of God's original champions and part of the angels who condemned and banned me for daring to question Heaven's authority."

I stared at the supposed angel intently, and he dropped his eyes of palest blue. "Are you telling me he's working for my uncle?"

That wouldn't go over well with my father.

"God is no longer my ruler. I left the kingdom of Heaven and pledged myself to the service of the One." Gabriel's expression turned dreamy, and his lips curved into a half smile, a vacant smile that made me shiver.

I hated fanatics. They always seemed to commit the most horrific crimes in the name of a higher power, and then, they had the nerve to question why they ended up in Hell.

"One who?" questioned Auric.

"Soon everybody will know the One's will, and the worlds above, below, and in between shall be remade."

Stupid cryptic answers. "Blah, blah, blah. What does that have to do with me?"

Eerie eyes peered into mine, and as I watched them cloud over, a chill swept through me.

Gabriel's mouth opened, but what emerged showed Gabriel was no longer home.

"Spawn of Satan, daughter of Earth—"

I interrupted. "Daughter of earth? Oh ew, please don't tell me my dad did it with a mud golem?" That was seriously twisted even for him.

The voice went on, but was it me or did it sound a touch irritated. "Lucifer's child, Gaia's progeny, heed my words. Your victory shall be short-lived. Your life even shorter. Pave the way for my arrival and perhaps you shall die quickly," said the puppet formerly known as Gabriel in a hissing whisper that sent icy fingers down my spine while, at the same time, making me wince as if nails were being dragged down a chalkboard.

The rebellious angel probably would have said more, but I'd always hated the part in the movies where bad guys got a monologue. No one needed to hear that crap.

With a swing of my sword, I decapitated Gabriel and watched dispassionately as his headless body tumbled to the floor.

Interestingly enough, no blood came out. An intriguing fact I didn't get to admire for long, as Gabriel's remains shrank in on themselves, getting smaller and smaller until, poof, he disappeared.

Sword sheathed, I turned to Auric with a bright smile. "Now that he's gone, shall we head on home and get naked?"

# CHAPTER SIXTEEN

Auric shook his head at me, but I could see the smile he tried to hide. "Baby, you are something else. I do wish, though, that you hadn't been so hasty. I still had some questions to ask him."

"Oh, please, I did everyone a favor. Who cares what that puppet had to say? He's dead, no longer a threat, so let's move on to more interesting stuff."

"Um, Muriel, didn't you hear what he said? He called you daughter of Gaia."

"Yeah, and I find that offensive. I am so definitely not gay. Like, hello, two male lovers."

Auric looked as though he might say something, but a commotion caught both our attention as a bleeding, black demon was thrown to his knees before us. David, still in panther form, loomed over Azazel, as did Chris whose staff smoked most interestingly.

"Traitor! You need to die," I snarled, reaching for my blade.

"Stop! He's mine," said my father in a booming voice. Daddy came striding through the ranks of his demon army. Dressed in black from his shining Hessian boots to his flowing, fur-edged cape. Finally, my dad had found a winter look that made him look menacing and impressive, even if it was somewhat Darth Vaderish.

I smiled at Azazel. "Guess you're too late for a quick death. Hope you enjoy your eternity of torture."

With a howl, Azazel was dragged by my father's minions to meet his punishment, which, knowing my dad, would be painful and, in this case, very deserving.

"Now are we done?" I asked impatiently. Auric came to stand behind me, and his warm body pressed against mine while his arms wrapped around me in a hug.

My father scowled. "No, you are not."

"What happened to great job, Muriel? Thanks for saving Hell."

"You killed a fallen angel. Big deal. But Hell is still in peril. You can leave as soon as you get the furnace going again."

"Me? Why can't one your mages do it?"

"Because I'm your father and I said so."

I pouted. "But I had other plans."

Auric whispered in my ear, "Are you sure you don't want to do it? You'll need lots of magic to light it."

I shivered, his innuendo clear. "Fine, I'll do it, but you all need to leave," I commanded, waving an imperious hand.

With some barked commands and a wink to me, my father had his demonic troops marching out of the chamber. Chris, with one arm wrapped around a limping Bambi's waist, gave us a wave and followed.

David swung his big feline head toward us for a moment then away, about to follow the others.

I looked up quickly at Auric, who nodded at me. "David, that didn't mean you," I shouted before he could leave.

I swear the giant kitty smiled. He padded back toward us, shifting back to his male form as he came, the sinuous muscles of his body as he moved making my heart speed faster.

Auric moved away for a moment. I turned to see why and saw him building a nest using his clothes in front of the cold furnace.

"Strip," he ordered.

"But it's cold," I complained, shivering.

"Not for long," he promised.

Hands pulled at my shirt, as David, not waiting for me, divested me of my clothing. When he knelt to remove my boots and pants, I knew he could smell my arousal because he rubbed his cheek against my creamy thigh, and even though he was human again, I swear I felt him purr.

Naked, David stood in front of me, his

erection poking and hot against my lower belly. Auric came up behind me, his hard length rubbing against my ass as he nuzzled my neck.

Sandwiched between their two naked bodies, the temperature in my body rose. Lips tasted the tender flesh of my neck, sucking and licking.

"Kiss her," ordered Auric.

David hesitated.

"Taste her," growled Auric.

I closed my eyes as David tentatively touched his lips to mine, his embrace soft and exploratory. Then another pair of lips took over. Auric. It wasn't hard to tell them apart. Auric had a fierceness to his embraces, and the touch of him always made my soul sing. David kissed more softly, savoring my lips like a fine wine that needed to be sipped slowly. And I enjoyed them both.

Arousal spun a web around us all. My limbs felt heavy, and Auric swept me up in his big arms, kissing me, and I found myself on the nest he had made. Auric lay down on one side of me, and his hot mouth left mine to lick and suck my taut nipple, a pleasure duplicated by David on the other side. I arched up, and two male hands were there to push me back down. Auric's rough fingers slid between my thighs, stroking me. He rolled on top of me, and I looked up into the face I loved dearly and gasped when he slid his hard length in. He pumped me with long, smooth strokes that made my pleasure swirl and build. I turned my head to the side and saw David watching us raptly, his hand stroking his cock. I beckoned him, wanting to feel him in my mouth. But he shook his head, eyes glittering and kept watching as Auric pumped me.

Determined to give him a better show, I pushed at Auric and mouthed, "On my knees." Before I'd even finished, I found myself flipped onto my stomach and Auric, with a hand curved around my waist, hauled me up so that my moist sex invited him. I heard David's breathing come more quickly, and I watched him with heavy lids as he fisted his cock, a sight I found exciting and erotic. Auric rubbed the tip of his velvety rod against my wet slit then rammed it in, making me cry out. I clawed at the piled clothing as Auric pounded my flesh, the sound of his body slapping mine loud. My hands were grabbed, and I opened my eyes to see David had finally moved. He placed my hands on his thighs, bringing me eye to eye with his swollen cock. My pussy squeezed Auric's shaft tightly, and I heard him groan and say, "Suck him. I want to see your head bobbing."

His order excited me, so I did as I was

told and took that swollen head between my lips. David's fingers wrapped themselves in my hair, and he controlled my motions. Slowed them. I wanted to suck him off fast, just like Auric fucked me now. But David had other ideas. He pushed his cock deep into my throat, almost gagging me with his length, then pulled it back a bit, slowly, before doing it again.

Behind me, Auric groaned, and his fingers dug into my waist as he slowed his pace to match David's, a pace that would surely drive me insane. By reducing the speed, they'd made sure I felt every single inch that slid in my mouth and sex. I could feel their cocks throbbing, and my pussy convulsed. Auric pushed his penis in deep, the tip brushing my womb, and he held it there, grinding his hips slightly, making me moan around David's shaft.

"Switch with me," grunted Auric.

Without a word, David pulled out of my mouth and switched spots with Auric. Auric took his place in front of me, his cock, so much thicker and slick with my juices, bobbing in front of me. I dove on it, sucking it hard. I bit down slightly when David penetrated me from behind, his penis jabbing me in my sweet spot and making me go wild. The two of them pumped me now, their breathing strained. As for me, I couldn't take it anymore and came—hard. My mouth screaming around Auric's cock, I orgasmed, my pussy muscles clenching David tightly, and with a hoarse cry, he came. I found myself on my back, my womb still quivering, when Auric, still hard, pushed my legs up over his shoulders and slid in. His thick cock made me cry out. My muscles tensed before coming again in a second orgasm that had me blacking out for a moment.

And the magic filled me up and kept filling me as Auric pumped me rhythmically, his face taut with strain.

"Now, Muriel. Use your power. Light that damned fire."

I wasn't sure how, but my magic screamed for release. With Auric still fucking me, and my pussy convulsing still with bliss, the magic kept pouring in. Amidst the ecstasy, the magic pulsed painfully.

Screaming, I threw my power at the furnace. For a moment, I saw a flicker.

"More," panted Auric, sweat beading his brow as he held back and drove himself in and out of my quivering body.

A hot mouth latched onto my nipple, licking and biting down, even as a finger found my clit and rubbed.

With a hoarse cry, I came again, the flood of magic racing through my body and directed out again to the furnace behind me.

More and more, I fed my power to the giant hearth, and just when I thought I wouldn't have enough magic, Auric finally came with a bellow, creaming me and making me come one last screaming time.

*Whoosh!*

The flames of Hell suddenly burst forth in the hearth, their instant warmth drying the sweat on our sated bodies.

But I'd used up a lot of energy, and with a sigh of pleasure, I passed out.

# CHAPTER SEVENTEEN

I regained consciousness snuggled between a pair of naked bodies. Exhausted but smiling, we dressed, although we left off the jackets and mitts. Hell had turned hot again.

Leaving the flames burning merrily, we exited the cavern but skipped the party back in the first circle. How could I tell there was a celebration going on? Because Daddy could never resist a chance to set off some fireworks.

But I wasn't in the mood, and luckily, neither was Auric because he opened a portal back to the apartment.

Immediately, I collapsed on the couch, exhausted and dirty. It could have been worse. At least we'd all survived. *Hell wins again!*

But with the threat gone, a certain someone shuffled his feet and wouldn't look at us. "I guess you don't need me anymore. I'll get going. See you around."

It broke my heart, and in that moment, I understood why Auric had asked that David join us. We'd been through a lot together in the last little bit. Auric had my soul, but David had stolen a piece of my heart, and I didn't like to see him looking lost and alone like this. And I knew neither did Auric.

Auric flashed me a glance and inclined his head, to which I responded with a smile.

"Stay," said my lover.

"Please," I added.

David finally lifted his head and looked at us. "Why?"

"Because you now belong with us. We need you. I need you." I held out my hand. Perhaps wanting to keep David made me a slut, but while I loved Auric with my entire being, a part of me loved David, too.

Screw what people thought and screw my previous morals. I was Lucifer's daughter, and selfishness ran in my genes. I wanted them both. David with his shy smiles but surprisingly hard core. And Auric, my very own fallen angel and consort.

Slowly David approached us, and I saw him look intently at Auric. I peeked up and saw Auric nod at him. David finally smiled and reached out to take my hand. Leading my men to the bathroom, I ordered them to strip.

About time I gave the orders around here.

It was a tighter fit in the shower with the three of us—I'd really need to look into getting this bathroom enlarged—but I quite enjoyed it. The guys made sure I stayed between them, an erotic delight that had me almost swooning as the feel of male flesh brushed me front and back.

Later that night, snuggled between their naked male bodies, I smiled contentedly.

Satan help me, but I loved them both. Even more wonderful, I knew they loved me, too.

# EPILOGUE

A few days later…

I had the three most important men in my life sitting down for a nice family dinner. My father was beaming since we'd just announced David had moved in.

"I can't believe it. My daughter living in sin with not one man but two. You do a father proud," Daddy said, toasting the occasion.

Auric rolled his eyes, used to my father's antics, but David looked taken aback. My father's sense of humor took getting used to for the uninitiated.

It had been almost a week now since we'd vanquished the hooded one. I still had a hard time thinking of him as Gabriel, another fallen angel, who was nothing like my precious Auric.

Auric had tried to bring up the subject of my mother a few times, but sticking my fingers in my ears and humming soon brought a stop to that. In the midst of the massive amount of magic I'd ingested, the pain blocks on that subject had thankfully been burned away, but my mind still remained a blank slate where she was concerned. Besides, I still had no interest in talking about the woman who'd birthed and left me. Not to mention fucked with my head.

Who did that? Certainly not someone I had any interest in.

My sister Bambi, despite her extensive wounds, had recovered by having marathon sex with a football team. Where other women might have found themselves traumatized by the violence, my poor sister just shrugged it off. Succubi often encountered angry wives and girlfriends, as well as jealous men. It made me sad that she'd come to expect that kind of treatment. What they'd put her through made me want to kill Gabriel again.

But I had killed the bastard. Hell was safe. Fist pump. Time to enjoy some naked time with my men.

A knock sounded at the door, not a pounding thump, and yet a knot formed in my stomach. Call it intuition, but I knew whoever stood on the other side was about to fuck up the nice new life I'd settled into.

"Don't answer," I said in a childish attempt to avoid whatever calamity waited for me on the other side.

At the look of worry on my face, Auric grabbed his holy sword before he headed for the door.

The person knocked a second time.

Auric yanked the door open, but his bulky body blocked my view so I couldn't see who'd come calling. And as if that weren't enough, David stood in front of me protectively. They still didn't get it that I could take care of myself.

I heard a chair go sliding back and hit the floor. I looked over to see my father staring at the door, stunned, his jaw dropped, shock on his face.

"No, it can't be," he muttered.

I needed to see what had my father looking like he'd seen a ghost. I walked around David, who, to my surprise, didn't try and stop me.

"Hello, Luc," said a petite woman, walking in. "It's been a long time."

Panic engulfed me for some reason, which made no sense. We'd cured the spell that had been causing the anxiety attacks. So what was happening?

I didn't know, and I didn't like it. I palmed my dinner knife.

"Do you know this woman, Daddy?" I asked, wondering why Auric had let this unknown woman in.

"Yes, and so do you," my father said. His expression was ashen.

I hated cryptic answers. They made my

head hurt. The woman, dressed in a nicely tailored green suit, stared at me. I rudely stared back, cataloguing her attributes from her long hair, lush figure, and oddly familiar face.

"Hello, Muriel. It's been a long time, my daughter."

The room spun, and I swooned. Thankfully there were several pairs of hands there to catch me.

I regained consciousness seated on Auric's lap with David handing me a glass of water, but I didn't dare grab it with my shaking hands.

The woman who'd come calling, also known as my mother, stood watching me enigmatically.

"What's your name?" I suddenly felt a monstrous need to know.

"I would have thought your first question would have been why I am here."

"Fine then, why are you here?"

"Why to witness the birth of your child. My grandchild. Which reminds me, congratulations to the fathers."

That did it. I threw the knife I still held in my hand.

## The End?

Not yet. The story continues in **Hell's Revenge.**

**Find out more at www.Evelanglais.com**

Printed in Great Britain
by Amazon